LOST ON THE MOON

Or, In quest of the field of diamonds

ROY ROCKWOOD

Lost On The Moon

Roy Rockwood

© 1st World Library, 2009
PO Box 2211 .
Fairfield, IA 52556
www.1stworldlibrary.com
First Edition

LCCN: 2009923498

Softcover ISBN: 978-1-4218-8881-1
Hardcover ISBN: 978-1-4218-8980-1
eBook ISBN: 978-1-4218-8782-1

Purchase *"Lost On The Moon"*
as a traditional bound book at:
www.1stWorldLibrary.com/purchase.asp?ISBN=978-1-4218-8881-1

1st World Library is a literary, educational organization
dedicated to:

- Creating a free internet library of downloadable ebooks

- Hosting writing competitions and offering book publishing
scholarships.

Interested in more 1st World Library books? contact:
literacy@1stworldlibrary.com
Check us out at: www.1stworldlibrary.com

1St World Library Literary Society

Giving Back to the World

"If you want to work on the core problem, it's early school literacy."

- James Barksdale, former CEO of Netscape

"No skill is more crucial to the future of a child, or to a democratic and prosperous society, than literacy."

- Los Angeles Times

"Literacy... means far more than learning how to read and write... The aim is to transmit... knowledge and promote social participation."

- UNESCO

"Literacy is not a luxury, it is a right and a responsibility. If our world is to meet the challenges of the twenty-first century we must harness the energy and creativity of all our citizens."

- President Bill Clinton

"Parents should be encouraged to read to their children, and teachers should be equipped with all available techniques for teaching literacy, so the varying needs and capacities of individual kids can be taken into account."

- Hugh Mackay

CONTENTS

CHAPTER I

A WONDERFUL STORY

"Well, what do you think of it, Mark?" asked Jack Darrow, as he laid aside a portion of a newspaper, covered with strange printed characters. "Great; isn't it?"

"You don't mean to tell me that you believe that preposterous story, do you, Jack?" And Mark Sampson looked across the table at his companion in some astonishment.

"Oh, I don't know; it may be true," went on Jack, again picking up the paper and gazing thoughtfully at it. "I wish it was."

"But think of it!" exclaimed Mark. "Why, if such a thing exists, and if we, or some one else, should attempt to bring all those precious stones to this earth, it would revolutionize the diamond industry of the world. It can't be true!"

"Well, here It is, in plain print. You can read it for yourself, as you know the Martian language as well as I do. It states that a large field of 'Reonaris' was discovered on the moon near Mare Tranquilitatis (or Tranquil Ocean, I suppose that could be translated), and that the men of Mars brought back some of the Reonaris with them. Here, read it, if you don't believe me."

"Oh, I believe you, all right—that is, I think you have translated that article as well as you can. But suppose you have made some error? We didn't have much time to study the language of Mars while we were there, and we might make some mistake in the words. That article might be an account of a dog-fight on the red planet, instead of an account of a trip to the moon and the discovery of a field of Reonaris; eh, Jack?"

"Of course, I'm likely to have made an error, for it isn't easy to translate this stuff." And Jack gazed intently at the strangely printed page, which was covered with characters not unlike Greek. "I may be wrong," went on the lad, "but you must remember that I translated some other articles in this paper, and Professor Henderson also translated them substantially as I did, and Professor Roumann agreed with him. There *is* Reonaris on the moon, and I wish we could go there and get some."

"But maybe after you got the Reonaris it would turn out to be only common crystals," objected Mark.

"No!" exclaimed Jack. "Reonaris is what the Martians call it in their language, and that means diamonds. I'm sure of it!"

"Well, I don't agree with you," declared the other lad.

"Don't be cranky and contrary," begged Jack.

"I'm not; but what's the use of believing anything so wild and weird as that? It's a crazy yarn!"

"It's nothing of the sort! There are diamonds on the moon; and I can prove it!"

"Well, don't get excited," suggested Mark calmly. "I don't believe it; that's all. You're mistaken about what Reonaris is; that's what you are."

"I am not!" Jack had arisen from his chair, and seemed much elated. In his hand he held clinched the paper which had caused the lively discussion. It was as near to a disagreement as Jack Darrow and Mark Sampson had come in some time.

"Sit down," begged Mark.

"I'll not!" retorted Jack. "I'm going to prove to you that I'm right."

"How are you going to do it?"

"I'm going to get Professor Henderson and Professor Roumann to translate this article for you, and then you can ask them what Reonaris is. Guess that'll convince you; won't it?"

"Maybe; but why don't you ask Andy Sudds or Washington White to give their opinion?"

"Don't get funny," advised the other lad sharply, and then, seeing that his chum was smiling, Jack laughed, cooled down a bit, looked at the paper which he had crumpled in his hand, and said:

"I guess I *was* getting a little too excited. But I'm sure I'm right. Here's the paper I brought from Mars to prove it, and the only thing there's any doubt about is whether or not Reonaris means diamonds. I'll ask—"

At that moment the door of the library, in which Jack and Mark were seated, was cautiously opened, and a black, woolly head was thrust in. Then two widely-opened eyes gazed at the boys.

"What's the matter, Washington?" asked Jack, with a laugh.

"'Scuse me, Massa Jack," answered the colored man, "but did I done heah you' to promulgate some conversationess regarding de transmigatorability ob diamonds?"

"Do you mean, were we talking about diamonds?" inquired Mark.

"Dat's what I done said, Massa Mark."

"No, you *didn't* say it, but you meant it, I guess," went on Jack. "Yes, we *were* talking about diamonds, Washington. I know a place that's full of them."

"Where?" inquired the colored man, thrusting his head farther into the room, and opening his eyes to their fullest extent. "Ef it ain't violatin' no confidences, Massa Jack, would yo' jest kindly mention it to yo's truly," and Professor Henderson's faithful servant, who had followed him into many dangers, looked at the two boys, who, of late years, had shared the labors of the well-known scientist. "Where am dose diamonds, Massa Jack?"

"On the moon," was the answer.

"On de moon? Ha! Ha! Dat's a joke!" And Washington began to laugh. "On de moon! Ha! Ho!"

"Well, you can read it for yourself," went on the lad, tossing the paper over to the colored man. The latter picked it up, gazed at it, first from one side, and then from the other. Next he turned it upside down, but, as this did not make the article

Roy Rockwood

any clearer, he turned the paper back again. Then he remarked, with a puzzled air:

"Well, I neber could read without mah glasses, Massa Jack, so I guess I'll hab t' let it go until annoder time. Diamonds on de moon, eh? Dat's wonderful! I wonder what dey'll be doin' next? But I'se got t' go. Diamonds on de moon, eh? Diamonds on de moon!"

As Washington turned to leave the room, for he had entered it when Jack and Mark were talking to aim, the latter lad asked:

"Did you want to see us about anything particular, Wash?"

"Why, I suah did," was the reply, "I did come t' tell yo' dat Perfesser Henderson would be pleased to hold some conversations wid yo', but when Massa Jack done mentioned about dem diamonds, I clean fo'got it. Diamonds on de moon, eh?"

"Well, if the professor wants us we'd better go," suggested Mark. "Come on, Jack, and stop dreaming about Reonaris and the moonbeams. Get back to earth."

"All right; laugh if you want to," said Jack sturdily, "but the time will come, Mark, when you'll find out that I'm right."

"How?" asked Mark.

"I don't know, but I'm sure I can prove what I say."

The two boys were to have the wonderful diamond story demonstrated to them sooner than either expected. Following the colored man, the lads, Jack carrying the paper, made their way to the laboratory of Professor Henderson. His door was open, and the aged man, whose hair and beard were now white with age, was bending over a table covered with papers, chemical apparatus, test tubes, alembecs, Bunsen burners, globes, and various pieces of apparatus. Another man, not quite so old as was Mr. Henderson, was on the point of leaving the apartment.

"Ah, boys," remarked the older professor, as he caught sight of them, "I hope I didn't disturb you by sending for you."

"No; Jack and I were only having a red-hot discussion about diamonds on the moon," said Mark, with a laugh.

"Diamonds on the moon!" exclaimed Professor Henderson.

"Diamonds on the moon?" repeated his friend, Prof. Santell Roumann. "Is this a joke, boys?"

"Mark thinks so, but I don't!" cried Jack, enthusiastically. "Look here, Professor Henderson, and also Mr. Roumann. Here is one of the newspapers that we brought back with us in our projectile, the *Annihilator*, after our trip to Mars. I have been translating some of the articles in it, and to-night I came across one that told of a trip made by some of the inhabitants of Mars to the moon, in a sort of projectile, like ours, only more on the design of an aeroplane.

"They landed on the moon, the article states, and found a big field, or deposit, of Reonaris, which I claim are diamonds. Mark says I'm wrong, but, Professor Henderson, isn't Reonaris to the Martians what diamonds are to us?"

"It certainly is," agreed the older scientist, and he looked for confirmation to his scholarly companion.

"Reonaris is substantially a diamond," said Professor

Roumann. "It has the same chemical constitution, and also the diamond's hardness and brilliancy. But I don't understand how any diamonds can be on the moon."

"You can read this for yourself," suggested Jack, passing over the paper, which was one of some souvenirs brought back from what was the longest journey on record, ever taken by human beings.

Mr. Roumann adjusted his glasses, and carefully read the article that was printed in such strange characters. As he perused it, he nodded his head thoughtfully from time to time. Then he passed the paper to Professor Henderson.

The older scientist was somewhat longer in going over the article, but when he had finished, he looked at the two boys, and said: "Jack is right! This is an account of a trip made to the moon by some of the Martians, who have advanced much further in the art of air navigation than have we. Some of the words I am not altogether familiar with, but in the main, that is what the paper states."

"And doesn't it tell about them finding a field of Reonaris?" asked Jack eagerly, for he was anxious to prove to his chum that he was right.

"Yes, it does," replied Mr. Henderson.

"And Reonaris is diamonds, isn't it?" asked Jack.

"It is," answered Professor Roumann gravely.

"Then," cried Jack, "what's to hinder us from going to the moon, and getting some of those diamonds? The Martians must have left some! Let's go to the moon and get them! We can do it in the projectile with which we made the journey to

Mars. Let's start for the moon!"

For a moment there was silence in the laboratory of the scientist. It was broken by Washington White, who remarked:

"Good land a' massy! Annodder ob dem trips through de air! Well, I ain't goin' to no moon—no sah!! Ef I went dere, I'd suah get looney, an' I has troubles enough now wid'out dat, I suah has!" And, shaking his head dubiously, the colored man shuffled from the room.

CHAPTER II

SOMETHING ABOUT OUR HEROES

"Are you in earnest in proposing this trip?" asked Professor Henderson of Jack. The lad, with flushed face and bright eyes, stood in the centre of the apartment, holding the paper which the aged scientist had returned to him.

"I certainly am," was the reply. "It ought not to be a difficult undertaking, after our trip to the North Pole through the air, the one to the South Pole under water, our journey to the centre of the earth, and our flight to Mars. Why, a trip to the moon ought to be a little pleasure jaunt, like an automobile tour. Can't we go, Professor?"

"From the standpoint of possibility, I presume we could make a trip to the moon," the scientist admitted. "It would not take so long, nor would it be as dangerous, as was our trip to Mars. And yet, I don't know that I care to go. I am getting along in years, and I have money enough to live on. Even a field of diamonds hardly sounds attractive to me." Jack's face showed the disappointment he felt.

"And yet," went on the aged scientist with a smile, "there are certain attractions about another trip through space. I had hoped to settle down in life now, and devote my time to scientific study and the writing of books. But this is something new. We never have been to the moon, and—"

"There are lots of problems about it that are still unsolved!" cried Jack eagerly. "You will be able to discover if the moon has an atmosphere and moisture; and also what the other side—the one that is always turned away from us—looks like."

"It does sound tempting," went on the aged scientist slowly. "And we could do it in our projectile, the *Annihilator*. It is in good working order; isn't it, Professor Roumann?"

"Couldn't be better. If you ask me, I, for one, would like to make a trip to the moon. It would give me a better chance to test the powers of Cardite, that wonderful red substance we brought from Mars. I can use that in the Etherium motor. If you left it to me, I'd say, 'go to the moon.'"

"Well, perhaps we will," spoke Mr. Henderson thoughtfully.

"You'll go, too, won't you, Mark?" asked Jack.

"Oh, I'm not going to be left behind. I'll go if the rest do, but I don't believe you'll find any diamonds on the moon. If there ever were any, the Martians took them." For Mark had been partly convinced after the confirmation by the two professors of Jack's translation.

"I'll take a chance on the sparklers," said his chum. "But now, let's go into details, and figure out when we can start. It ought not to take very long to get ready."

As has been explained in detail in the other books of this series, Professor Amos Henderson and the two lads, Mark Sampson and Jack Darrow, had undertaken many strange voyages together. Sometimes they were accompanied by friends and assistants, while Washington White, a sort of servant, helper, and man-of-all-work, and Andy Sudds, an old hunter, always went with them.

Mark and Jack were orphans, who had been adopted by Professor Henderson, who spent all his time making wonderful machines for transportation, or conducting strange experiments.

The two boys had been rescued by Professor Henderson and Washington White from a train wreck. Although both boys were badly hurt, they were nursed back to health by the eminent scientist, who soon learned to care for the lads as though they had been his own sons.

They aided the professor, as soon as they were able, in constructing an airship, called the *Electric Monarch*, in which Professor Henderson hoped to be able to reach the North Pole. The boys thoroughly enjoyed the trip through the air, and had many thrills fighting the savage Eskimos. Finally, they succeeded in passing over the exact spot of the North Pole during a violent snowstorm.

Not satisfied with their experiences after conquering the North, the adventurers set out for the Antarctic regions in a submarine boat. This trip, even more remarkable than the first, took them to many strange places in the South Atlantic. They were trapped for a time in the Sargasso Sea, and they walked on the ocean floor in new diving suits, one of the professor's marvelous inventions.

It was on the voyage to the south that, coming to the surface one day, the adventurers saw a strange island in the Atlantic Ocean, far from the coast of South America. On it was a great whirlpool, into which the *Porpoise*, their submarine boat, was nearly drawn by the powerful suction.

The chasm might lead to the center of the earth, it was suggested, and, after thinking the matter over, on their return from the Antarctic, Professor Henderson decided to build a craft in which they might solve the mystery.

The details of the voyage they took in the *Flying Mermaid*, are told of in the third volume, entitled "Five Thousand Miles Underground." The *Mermaid* could sail on the water, or float in the air like a balloon. In this craft the travellers descended into the centre of the earth, and had many wonderful adventures. They nearly lost their lives, and had to escape, after running through danger of the spouting water, leaving their craft behind.

For some time they undertook no further voyages, and the two boys, who lived with Professor Henderson in a small town on the coast of Maine, were sent to attend the Universal Electrical and Chemical College. Washington remained at home to minister to the wants of the old professor, and Andy Sudds went off on occasional hunting trips.

But the spirit of adventure was still strong in the hearts of the boys and the professor. One day, in the midst of some risky experiments at college, Jack and Mark, as related in "Through Space to Mars," received a telegram from Professor Henderson, calling them home.

There they found their friend entertaining as a guest Professor Santell Roumann, who was almost as celebrated as was Mr. Henderson, in the matter of inventions.

Professor Roumann made a strange proposition. He said if the old scientist and his young friends would build the proper kind of a projectile, they could make a trip to the planet

Mars, by means of a wonderful motor, operated by a power called Etherium, of which Mr. Roumann held the secret.

After some discussion, the projectile, called the *Annihilator*, from the fact that it annihilated space, was begun. It was two hundred feet long, ten feet in diameter in the middle, and shaped like a cigar. It consisted of a double shell of strong metal, with a non-conducting gas between the two sides.

Within it were various machines, besides the Etherium motor, which would send the projectile along at the rate of one hundred miles a second. This great speed was necessary in order to reach the planet Mars, which, at the time our friends started for it, was about thirty- five millions of miles away from this earth. It has since receded some distance farther than this.

Finally all was in readiness for the start to Mars. Professor Roumann wanted to prove that the planet was inhabited, and he also wanted to get some of a peculiar substance, which he believed gave the planet its rosy hue. He had an idea that it would prove of great value.

But, though every precaution was taken, the adventurers were not to get away from the earth safely. Almost at the last minute, a crazy machinist, named Fred Axtell, who was refused work on the projectile, tried to blow it up with a bomb. He partly succeeded, but the damage was repaired, and the start made.

Inside the projectile our friends shut themselves up, and the powerful motors were started. Off it shot, at the rate of one hundred miles a second, but the travellers were as comfortable as in a Pullman car. They had plenty to eat and drink, they manufactured their own air and water, and they slept when they so desired.

But Axtell, the crazy machinist, had hidden himself aboard, and, in mid-air, he tried to wreck the projectile. He was caught, and locked up in a spare room, but, when Mars was reached, he escaped.

The book tells how our friends were welcomed by the Martians, how they learned the language, saw many strange sights, and finally got on the track of the Cardite, or red substance, which the German professor, Mr. Roumann, had come so far to seek. This Cardite was capable of great force, and, properly controlled, could move great weights and operate powerful machinery.

Our friends wanted to take some back to earth with them, but when they attempted to store it in their projectile, they met with objections, for the Martians did not want them to take any. They had considerable trouble, and the crazy machinist led an attack of the soldiers of the red planet against our friends, the adventurers in the projectile.

Among the other curiosities brought away by our friends, was a newspaper printed in Mars, for the inhabitants of that place where much further advanced along certain lines than we are on this earth, but in the matter of newspapers they had little to boast of, save that the sheets were printed by wireless electricity, no presses being needed.

As told at the opening of this story, Jack had noticed on one of the sheets they brought back, an account of how some of the Martians made a trip to the moon, and discovered a field of Reonaris. This trip was made shortly before our friends made their hasty departure, and it was undertaken by some Martian adventurers on another part of the red planet than where the projectile landed, and so Professor Henderson and his friends did not hear of it at the time.

"Well, then, suppose we make the attempt to go to the moon," said Professor Roumann, after a long discussion in the laboratory. "It will not take long to get ready."

"I'd like to go," said Jack. "How about you, Professor Henderson? Oh, by the way, Washington said you wanted to see Mark and me, but I was so interested in this news item, that I forgot to ask what it as about."

"I merely wanted to inquire when you and Mark thought of resuming your studies at college," said the aged man, "but, since this matter has come up, it will be just as well if you do not arrange to resume your lessons right away."

"We can study while making the trip to the moon," suggested Mark.

"Not much," declared Jack, with a laugh. "There'll be too much to see."

"Well, we'll discuss that later," went on Mr. Henderson. "Practically speaking, I think the voyage can be made, and, the more I think of it, the better I like the idea. We will look over the projectile in the morning, and see what needs to be done to it to get it ready for another trip through space."

"Not much will have to be done, I fancy," remarked the German scientist. "But I want to make a few improvements in the Cardite motor, which I will use in place of the Etherium one, that took us to Mars."

A little later there came a knock on the rear door of the rambling old house where the professor lived and did much of his experimental work.

"I'll go," volunteered Jack, and when he opened the portal

there stood on the threshold a small boy, Dick Johnson, one of the village lads.

"What is it you want, Dick?" asked Mark.

"Here's a note for you," went on the boy, passing over a slip of paper. "I met a man down the road, and he gave me a quarter to bring it here. He said it was very important, and he's waiting for you down by the white bridge over the creek."

"Waiting for who?" asked Jack.

"For Mark, I guess; but I don't know. Anyhow, the note's for him."

"Hum! This is rather strange," mused Mark.

"What is it?" asked Jack.

"Why, this note. It says: 'It is important that I see you. I will wait for you at the white bridge.' That's all there is to it."

"No name signed?" asked Jack.

"Not a name. But I'll just take a run down and see what it is. I'll not be long. Much obliged, Dick."

The boy who had brought the note turned to leave the house, and Mark prepared to follow. Jack said:

"Let me see that note."

He scanned it closely, and, as Mark was getting on his hat and coat, for the night was chilly, his chum went on:

Roy Rockwood

"Mark, if I didn't know, that we had left Axtell, the crazy machinist, up on Mars, I'd say that this was his writing. But, of course, it's impossible."

"Of course—impossible," agreed Mark.

"But, there's one thing, though," continued Jack.

"What's that?" asked Mark.

"I don't like the idea of you going off alone in the dark, to meet a man who doesn't sign his name to the note he wrote. So, if you have no objections, I'll go with you. No use taking any chances."

"I don't believe I run any risk," said Mark, "but I'll be glad of your company. Come along. Maybe it's only a joke." And the two lads started off together in the darkness toward the white bridge.

CHAPTER III

PREPARING FOR A VOYAGE

"Seems like rather an odd thing; doesn't it?" remarked Jack, as he and his chum walked along.

"What?"

"This note."

"Oh, yes. But what made you think the writing looked like that of the crazy machinist who tried to wreck the projectile?"

"Because I once saw some of the crazy letters he sent us, and he wrote just like the man who gave Dick this note. But come on, let's hustle, and see what's up."

In a few minutes they came in sight of the white bridge, which was about a quarter of a mile down the road from the professor's house. The two boys kept well together, and they were watching for a first sight of the man in waiting.

"See anything?" asked Jack.

"No; do you?"

"Not a thing. Wait until we get closer. He may be in the shadow. It's dark now."

Almost as Jack spoke, the moon, which had been hidden behind a bank of clouds, peeped out, making the scene comparatively bright. The boys peered once more toward the bridge, and, as they did so, they saw a figure step from the shadows, stand revealed for an instant in the middle of the structure, and then, seemingly after a swift glance toward the approaching chums, the person darted off in the darkness.

"Did you see that?" cried Jack.

"Sure," assented Mark. "Guess he didn't want to wait for us. Why, he's running to beat the band!"

"Let's take after him," suggested Jack, and, nothing loath, Mark assented. The two lads broke into a run, but, as they leaped forward, the man also increased his pace, and they could hear his feet pounding out a tattoo on the hard road.

The two youths reached the bridge, and sped across it. They glanced hastily on either side, thinking possibly the man might have had some companions, but no one was in sight, and the stranger himself was now out of view around a bend in the highway.

"No use going any farther," suggested Jack, pulling up at the far side of the bridge. "There are two roads around the bend, and we couldn't tell which one he'd take. Besides, it might not be altogether safe to risk it."

Mark and Jack, on their return, told Professor Henderson and the German scientist something of their little excursion.

"But who could he have been?" asked Mr. Roumann.

"Perhaps if you ask the boy who brought the note he can tell you."

"We'll do it in the morning," decided Mark.

"It's peculiar that he wanted Mark to meet him," spoke Amos Henderson. "Have you any enemies that you know of, Mark?"

"Not a one. But what makes you think this man was an enemy, Professor?"

"From the fact that he ran when he saw you and Jack together. Evidently he expected to get Mark out alone."

They discussed the matter for some time, and then the boys and the scientists retired to bed, ready to begin active preparations on the morrow, for their trip to the moon.

There was much to be done, but their experience in making other wonderful trips, particularly the one to Mars, stood the travellers in good stead. They knew just how to go to work.

To Washington was entrusted the task of preparing the food supply, since he was to act as cook. Andy Sudds was instructed to look after the clothing and other supplies, except those of a scientific nature, while the two young men were to act as general helpers to the two professors.

As the *Annihilator* has been fully described in the volume entitled, "Through Space to Mars," there is no need to dwell at any length on the construction of the projectile in which our friends hoped to travel to the moon. Sufficient to say that it was a sort of enclosed airship, capable of travelling through space—that is, air or ether—at enormous speed, that there were contained within it many complicated machines, some for operating the projectile, some for offence or defence against enemies, such as electric guns, apparatus for making air or water, and scores of scientific instruments.

The *Annihilator* was controlled either from the engine room, or from a pilot house forward. As for the motive power it was, for the trip to the moon, to be of that wonderful Martian substance, Cardite, which would operate the motors.

The projectile moved through space by the throwing off of waves of energy, similar to wireless vibrations, from large plates of metal, and these plates were the invention of Professor Roumann.

Perhaps to some of my readers it may seem strange to speak so casually of a trip to the moon, but it must be remembered that our friends had already accomplished a much more difficult journey, namely, that to Mars. So the moon voyage was not to daunt them.

Mars, as I have said, was thirty-five millions of miles away from the earth when the *Annihilator* was headed toward it. To reach the moon, however, but 252,972 miles, at the most, must be traversed—a little more than a quarter of a million miles. As the distance from the earth to the moon varies, being between the figures I have named, and 221,614 miles, with the average distance computed as being 238,840 miles, it can readily be seen that at no time was the voyage to be considered as comparing in distance with the one to Mars.

But there were other matters to be taken into consideration, and our friends began to ponder on them in the days during which they made their preparations.

CHAPTER IV

AN ACCIDENT

Washington White was kept busy getting together the food for the voyage, and he had about completed his task, while Andy Sudds announced one morning that his department was ready for inspection, and that he thought he would go hunting until the projectile was ready to start.

"Well, if you see anything of that queer man who sent me the note, just ask him what he meant by it," suggested Mark, for inquiry from the boy who had brought the message, developed the fact that Dick did not know the man, nor had he ever seen him before. He was a stranger in the neighborhood. But, as nothing more resulted from it, the two lads gave the matter no further thought.

"How soon before we will be ready to start?" asked Jack one day, while he and his chum, with the two professors, were working over the projectile, which was soon to be shot through space.

"In about two weeks," replied Mr. Roumann. "I want to make a few changes in the Cardite plates, which will replace the ones used on the Etherium motor. Then I want to test them, and, if I find that they work all right, as I hope, we will seal ourselves up in the *Annihilator*, and start for the moon."

"Are you going to try to go around it, and land on the side turned away from us?" asked Mark, who had been studying astronomy lately.

"What do you mean by that?" asked Jack. "Doesn't the moon turn around?"

"Not as the earth does," replied his chum; "or, rather, to be more exact, it rotates exactly as the earth does, on its axis; but, in doing this it occupies precisely the same time that it takes to make a revolution about our planet. So that, in the long run, to quote from my astronomy, it keeps the same side always toward the earth; and today, or, to be more correct, each night that the moon is visible, we see the same face and aspect that Galileo did when he first looked at it through his telescope, and, unless something happens, the same thing will continue for thousands of years."

"Then we've never seen the other side of the moon?" asked Jack.

"Never; and that's why I wondered if the professor was going to attempt to reach it. Perhaps there are people there, and air and water, for it is practically certain that there is neither moisture nor atmosphere on this side of Luna."

"Wow! Then maybe we'd better not go," said Jack, with a shiver. "What will we do, if we get thirsty?"

"Oh, I guess we can manage, with all the apparatus we have, to distill enough water," said Professor Henderson, with a smile. "Then, too, we will take plenty with us, and, of course, tanks of oxygen to breathe. But it will be interesting to see if there are people on the moon."

"If there are any, they must have a queer time," went on Mark.

"Why?" asked Jack, who wasn't very fond of study.

"Why? Because the moon is only about one forty-ninth the size of the earth. Its diameter is 2,163 miles—only a quarter of the earth's—and, comparing the force of gravity, ours is much greater. A body that weighs six pounds on the earth, would weigh only one pound on the moon, and a man on the moon could jump six times as high as he can on this earth, and throw a stone six times as far."

"What's dat?" inquired Washington White quickly, nearly dropping some packages he was carrying into the projectile. "What was yo' pleased t' saggasiate, in remarkin' concernin' de untranquility ob the densityness ob stones jumpin' ober a man what is six times high?" he asked.

"Do you mean what did I say?" asked Mark solemnly.

"Dat's what I done asked yo'," spoke the colored man gravely.

"Well, you didn't, but perhaps you meant to," went on the youth, and he repeated his remarks.

"'Scuse me, I guess I'd better not go on dish yeah trip after all," came from Washington.'

"Why not?" demanded Professor Henderson.

"'Cause I ain't goin' t' no place whar ef yo' wants t' take a little jump yo' has t' go six times as far as yo' does when yo' is on dis yeah earth. An' s'posin' some ob dem moon men takes a notion t' throw a stone at me? Whar'll I be, when a stone goes six times as far as it does on heah? No, sah, I ain't goin'!"

"But perhaps there are no men on the moon," said Mark quickly. "It is only a theory of astronomers that I'm talking about."

"Oh, only a theory; eh?" asked Washington quickly.

"That's all."

"Oh, if it's only a theory, den I reckons it's all right," came from the colored man. "I didn't know it were a theory. Dat makes it all right. It's jest in theory, am it, Massa Mark, dat a stone goes six times as far?"

"That's all."

"Oh, well, den, why didn't yo' say so fust, dat it was only a theory? I don't mind theories. I—I used t' eat 'em boiled an' roasted befo' de wah." And, with a contented smile on his face, Washington went into the projectile, to finish stowing things away in his kitchen lockers.

The big projectile was housed in the shed where it had been constructed, and the professor and the boys were working over it there, carefully guarded from curious eyes, for the German inventor did not want the secret of his Cardite motor to become known.

The work went on from day to day, good progress being made. The boys were of great assistance, for they were practical mechanics, and had had considerable experience.

"Well, I shall try the Cardite motor to-morrow," announced Professor Roumann one night, after a hard day's work on the projectile.

"Do you think it will work?" asked Mr. Henderson.

"I think so, yes. My experiments have made me hopeful."

"And if it does work, when can we start?" asked Jack.

"Two days later; that is, if everything else is in readiness, the food and other, supplies on board."

"They are all ready to be stowed away," said Andy Sudds, who had been hunting all day.

It was an anxious assemblage that gathered inside the big shed the next day, to watch Professor Roumann try the Cardite motor. Would it work as well as had the Etherium one? Would it send them along through space at enormous speed? True, they would not have to travel so far, nor so fast, but more power would be needed, since, as it was feared no food, water, nor air could be had on the moon, many more supplies were to be taken along than on the trip to Mars, and this made the projectile heavier.

"We will test the Cardite in this small motor first," said Mr. Roumann, as he pointed to a machine in the projectile used for winding a cable around a windlass when there was necessity for hauling the *Annihilator* about, without sending it into the air.

Into the receptacle of the motor, the German professor placed some of the wonderful red substance he had secured from Mars. Then he closed the heavy metal box that held it, and, looking about to see if all was in readiness, he motioned to those watching him that he was about to shift the lever that would start the motor.

"If it works as well as I hope it will," he said, "it ought to pull the projectile slowly across the shop—a task that would be impossible in a motor of this size, if operated by electricity, gasoline, or any other force at present in use. And, if this small motor will do that, I know the large ones will send us through space to the moon. All ready, now."

Slowly the professor shoved over the lever, while Jack, Mark and the others watched him carefully. They were standing back of him, in the engine room of the projectile.

There was a clicking sound as the lever snapped into place. This was succeeded by a buzzing hum, as the motor began to absorb the great power from the red substance, which was not unlike radium in its action. There was a trembling to the great projectile.

"She's moving!" cried Jack.

Hardly had he spoken when there was a flash of red fire, a sound as of a bursting bomb, and everyone was knocked from his feet, over backward, while Professor Roumann was hurled the entire length of the engine room.

"The Cardite motor has exploded!" cried Mark. "Professor Roumann is killed!"

CHAPTER V

THE WORK OF AN ENEMY

Jack's first act, on arising from amid a mass of tools, into which he had been tossed by the explosion, was to run to where Professor Roumann lay in a semi-conscious condition. An instant later Mark slowly arose, and made his way to where Professor Henderson was rubbing his forehead in a dazed fashion.

"Are you hurt?" asked Mark, of his aged friend.

"I think not," answered Mr. Henderson slowly, "but I fear Mr. Roumann is. See to him; I'm all right."

"He's breathing," cried Jack, who had bent over the German. "He isn't dead, at any rate."

"But he may be, unless he gets attention," said Professor Henderson. "Get my medicine chest, Mark, and we'll see what we can do for him."

Jack had raised the head of the injured man on his arm, and was giving him some water from a glass. This partially revived the German, and he opened his eyes. He looked around, into the faces of his friends, as if scarcely comprehending what had happened, and then, as his gaze wandered toward the disabled Cardite motor, he exclaimed:

"Some enemy has done this! The motor was tampered with. The resistance block was loosened, and that caused the force of the Cardite to shoot out at the rear. We must watch out for the work of this enemy!"

"Don't distress yourself about that now," urged Mr. Henderson. "Are you badly hurt? Do you need a doctor?"

The German slowly drank the rest of the water which Jack gave him, and then gradually arose to a standing position.

"I am all right," he said faintly, "except that I feel a trifle dizzy. Something hit me on the head, and the fumes from the Cardite took away my breath for a moment. I think I shall be all right soon."

"Here is the medicine chest!" exclaimed Mark, coming back into the engine room. Mr. Henderson poured out some aromatic spirits of ammonia into a graduated glass, added a little water, and gave it to his fellow, inventor, who, after drinking it, declared that he felt much better. There was a cut on his forehead, where a piece of the broken motor had struck him, but, otherwise, he did not seem injured externally.

As for the boys, they were only stunned, nor was Mr. Henderson more than momentarily shocked. In a few minutes the German professor was almost himself again.

"We must try to discover who our enemy is," he said earnestly, as he looked over the disabled motor. "He might have blown up the whole projectile by tampering as he did with the machinery. Had I been testing the large, instead of the small motor, there would have been nothing left of the *Annihilator*, or us, either. Who could have done this? If that crazy machinist is around again—"

"I don't believe he could get here from Mars," interrupted Jack, with a smile.

"Hardly," added Mark.

"No, I guess he is still on the Red Planet, so it couldn't have been him," went on Mr. Roumann. "But it was some one."

Jack and Mark at once thought of the odd man who had sent Mark the note, and then had run away.

"Could it have been him?" suggested Jack.

"It's possible," remarked Professor Henderson. "We must be on our guard. I wonder if Washington—"

At that moment there sounded a violent pounding on the exterior of the projectile, and the voice of the colored man could be heard calling:

"Am anything de mattah? Andy Sudds an' I is out heah, an' we heard suffin goin' on in dere. Am anybody hurted?"

"It's all over now, Wash," replied Jack, for the two boys, and the two professors, had shut themselves up in the projectile while they conducted the experiment. Jack opened the door of the *Annihilator* and stepped out, being met by the colored man and the old hunter.

"You haven't seen any suspicious characters around, have you, Wash?" asked Mark. "Some one has been tampering with a motor, and it exploded."

"Nobody's been around since I've been here," announced Andy Sudds, with a significant glance at his gun.

"Maybe it's some ob dem moon-men, what don't laik de idea ob us goin' dere arter dere diamonds," volunteered the colored man.

"Perhaps," admitted Jack, with a smile. "But certainly some one has been around here who had no business to be, and we must find out who it was. Better take a look around, Wash."

"I'll help him," said Andy, and, with his rifle in readiness for any intruders, the old hunter followed the colored man outside the big shed.

Meanwhile Professor Roumann and Mr. Henderson were carefully examining the exploded motor.

"I should have looked at the breech plug before turning on the power," said the German, "but I had no reason to suspect that anything was wrong." He went on to explain that the explosion was something like that which occurs when the breech-block of a big navy gun is not properly in place. The force of the Cardite, instead of being directed against the piston-heads of the motor, shot out backward, and almost into the face of the professor, who was operating the machine.

"But what could be their object?" asked Mark. "Who would want to injure us, or damage the projectile?"

"Some enemy, of course," declared Jack. "But who? The crazy machinist is out of it, and as for that man who sent the note to you, he seemed too big a coward to attempt anything like this."

"Some one evidently sneaked in here and loosened the breech-plug," went on Mark, "and it was evidently done with the idea of delaying us. The enemy could not have desired to utterly disable the projectile, or else he would have tampered with the large motor, instead of the small one."

"Yes, the object seems to have been to delay us," admitted Professor Henderson; "yet, I can't understand why. Whoever did it evidently knows something about machinery."

"I hope they did not discover the secret of my Cardite motor," said Professor Roumann quickly.

"They hardly had time," declared Mark. "We have been in or around the projectile nearly every minute of the day, and whoever it was, must have watched his chance, slipped in, stayed a few seconds, and then slipped out again."

They went carefully over the entire projectile, but could find no further damage done. Nor were there any traces of the person who had so nearly caused a tragedy. Washington and Andy, after a careful search outside the shed, had to admit that they had no clews.

"Well, the only thing to do is to go to work and build a new small motor," announced Professor Roumann, after once more looking over the *debris* of the one that had exploded.

"Will it take long?" asked Jack.

"About two weeks. Fortunately, I can use some of the parts of this one, or we would be delayed longer."

"Still two weeks is quite a while," suggested Mark. "Perhaps there'll be no diamonds left on the moon when we get there, Jack," and he smiled jokingly.

"Oh, I fancy there will. The article in the paper from Mars says there was a whole field of them."

"This brings up another matter," said Professor Henderson. "What will happen if we bring back bushels and bushels of diamonds?—which, in view of what the paper says, may be possible. We will swamp the market, and the value of diamonds will drop."

"Then we must not throw them upon the market," decided Professor Roumann. "The scarcity of an article determines its value. If we do find plenty of diamonds, it will give me a chance to conduct some experiments I have long postponed because of a lack of the precious stones. We can use them for laboratory purposes, and need not sell them. In fact, with the Cardite we brought back from Mars, we have no lack of money, so we really do not need the diamonds."

It was decided, in view of the shock and upset caused by the explosion, that no further work would be done that day, and so, after carefully locking the shed, and posting Andy on guard with his gun, the boys and the professor went into the house to discuss matters, and plan for work the next day.

"Mark," said Jack in a low voice, as they followed the two scientists, "I think it's up to us to try to find that mysterious man who sent the note. I think he did this mean trick!"

"So do I, and we'll have a hunt for him. Let's go now."

CHAPTER VI

ON THE TRACK

The two boys gazed after Professors Henderson and Roumann. The scientists were deep in a discussion of various technical matters, which discussion, it was evident, made them oblivious to everything else.

"Shall we ask them?" inquired Jack in a whisper.

"No; what's the use?" queried Mark. "Let's go off by ourselves, and perhaps we can discover something. If we could once get on the trail of the man who wrote the note, I think we could put our hands on the person responsible for the blowing up of the motor."

"I agree with you. We won't bother them about our plans," and he waved his hand toward the scientists, who had, by this time, entered the house.

"In the first place," said Mark, as he and his chum turned from the yard, and walked along a quiet country road, "I think our best plan will be to find Dick Johnson, and ask him just where it was he met the man who gave him a quarter to bring the note to me."

"What for?" asked Jack.

"Why, then, we can tell where to start from. Perhaps Dick can give us a description of the man, or tell from what direction he came. Then we'll know how to begin on the trail."

"That's a good idea, I guess. We know where he disappeared to, or, rather, in nearly what direction, so that will help some."

"Sure. Well, then, let's find Dick."

To the inquiries of the two lads from the projectile, Dick Johnson replied that, as he had asserted once before, that the man was a stranger to him.

"He was tall, and had a big black mustache," Dick described, "but he kept his hat pulled down over his eyes, so I couldn't see his face very well. Anyhow, it was dark when I met him."

"Where did you meet him?" asked Mark.

"Not far from your house. He was standing on the corner, where you turn down to go to the woollen mill, and, as I passed him, he asked me if I wanted to earn a quarter."

"Of course you said you did," suggested Jack.

"Sure," replied Dick. "Then he gave me the note, and told me where to take it, and I did. That wasn't wrong, was it?"

"No; only there seems to be something queer about the man, and we want to find out what it is," replied Mark.

"What was the man doing when you saw him?" asked Jack.

"Standing, and sort of looking toward your house."

"Looking toward our house?" repeated Jack. "Was he anywhere near the big shed where we build the machines?"

"Well, I couldn't say. Maybe he might have been."

"I guess that's all you can tell us," put in Mark, with a glance at his chum, to warn him not to go too much into details with Dick, for they did not want it known that some enemy had tried to wreck the projectile.

"Yes, I can't tell you any more," admitted the small lad.

"Well, here's a quarter for what you did tell us," said Jack, "and if you see that man again, and he gives you a note for us, just keep your eye on him, watch where he goes, and tell us. Then you will get a half- dollar."

"Gee! I'll be on the watch," promised Dick, his eyes shining at the prospect of so much money.

"Come on," suggested Jack to his chum, after the small chap had departed. "Let's go down by the white bridge and make some inquiries of people living in that vicinity. They may have seen a stranger hanging around, and, perhaps we can get on his trail that way."

"All right," agreed Mark, and they walked on together.

They had gone quite a distance away from the bridge, and had made several inquiries, but had met with no success, and they were about to give up and go back home.

"I know one person we haven't inquired of yet," said Mark, as they tramped along.

"Who's that?"

"Old Bascomb, who lives alone in a shack on the edge of the creek. You know the old codger who traps muskrats."

"Oh, sure; but I don't believe he'd know anything. If he did, he's so cranky he wouldn't tell you."

"Maybe he would, if we gave him a little money for some smoking tobacco. It's worth trying, anyhow. Bascomb goes around a great deal, and he may have met a strange man in his travels."

"Well, go ahead; we'll ask him."

The muskrat trapper did not prove to be in a very pleasant frame of mind, but, after Mark had given him a quarter, Bascomb consented to answer a few questions. The boys told him about looking for a strange man, describing him as best they could, though they did not tell why they wanted to find him.

"Wa'al, now, I shouldn't be surprised but what I know the very fellow you want," said the trapper. "I met him a couple of days back, an' I think he's still hanging around. Fust I thought he was after some of my traps, but when I found he wa'ant, I didn't pay no more attention to him. He looked jest like you say."

"Where was he?" asked Jack eagerly.

"Walkin' along the creek, sort of absent-minded like."

"You don't know where he lives, or whether he is staying in this vicinity, do you?" inquired Mark.

"Ya'as, I think I do," replied the trapper.

"Where?" cried Jack eagerly.

"Wa'al, you know the old Preakness homestead, down by the bend of the creek, about four mile below here?"

"Sure we know it," answered Mark. "We used to go in swimming not far from there."

"Wa'al, the old house has been deserted now for quite a spell," went on the trapper, "and there ain't nobody lived in it but tramps. But the other night, when I was comin' past, with a lot of rats I'd jest taken out of my traps, I see a light in the old house. Thinks I, to myself, that there's more tramps snoozin' in there, and I didn't reckon it was none of my business, so I kept on. But jest as I was walking past the main gate, some one come out of the house and hurried away. I had a good look at him, an'—"

"Who was it?" asked Mark impatiently, for the old trapper was a slow talker.

"It was the same man you're lookin' for," declared Bascomb. "I'm sure of it, an' he's hangin' out in the old Preakness house. If you want t' see him, why don't you go there?"

"We will!" cried Jack. "Come on, Mark. I think we're on the trail at last."

CHAPTER VII

MARK IS CAPTURED

Eagerly the boys hurried forward, intent on making the best time possible to the old Preakness homestead, which was a landmark for miles around, and which, in its day, had been a handsome house and estate. Now it was fallen into ruins, for there was a dispute among the heirs, and the property was in the Chancery Court.

"Do you think we'll find him there?" asked Mark, as they made their way along the dusty highway. "Hard to tell. Yet, if he's hanging out in this neighborhood, that would be as good a place as any, for him to hide in."

"I wonder who he can be, anyhow? And how he knows me?"

"Give it up. Evidently he isn't a tramp, though he stays in a place where there are plenty of the Knights of the Road."

The boys increased their pace, and were soon on the main road leading to the Preakness house, and about a mile away from it. "We'll soon be there now," remarked Jack. "Then we'll see if we can find that man."

As he spoke, the lad put his hand in his pocket, and, a

moment later, he uttered a startled cry.

"What's the matter?" asked Mark, in some alarm.

"Matter? Why, gee whiz! If I haven't forgotten to send that telegram Professor Henderson gave me! It's to order some special tools to take along on our trip to the moon. They didn't come, and the professor wrote out a message urging the factory to hurry the shipment. He gave it to me to send, just before the accident to the motor, but when that happened it knocked it out of my mind, I guess. I stuck the telegram in my pocket, and here it is yet," and Jack drew forth a crumpled paper. "Wouldn't that make you tired?" he asked. "It's important, and ought to go at once. The professor won't like it."

"I'll tell you what to do," suggested Mark, after a moment's thought. "The telegraph office isn't so far away from here. You can cut across lots, and be there in fifteen or twenty minutes. Tell 'em to rush the message, and it may be in time yet. Anyhow, we're going to be delayed because of the accident to the motor, so it won't make so much difference. But come on, let's start, and we can hurry back."

"I guess that's the best plan," remarked Jack dubiously, for he did not fancy a half-hour's tramp across the fields and back again. Then, as he thought of something else, he called out:

"Say, Mark, there's no use of both of us going to the telegraph office. I'll go alone, as it's my fault, and you can stay here, and watch to see if that strange man appears on the scene. I'll not be long, and you can wait for me here."

"How would it be if I went on a little nearer to the Preakness house?" asked Mark. "I can meet you there just as well as here, and something may develop."

"Good idea! You go on, and when I come back, I'll take the road that leads through the old slate quarry, and save some time that way. I'll meet you right near the old barn that stands on the Gilbert property, just before you reach the Preakness grounds."

"All right; I'll be there, but don't run your legs off. We're out for all day, and there isn't anything that needs to be done at home, or around the projectile, so take your time."

"Oh, I'll not go to sleep," declared Jack. "I want to see if we can't solve the mystery of the man who writes such queer notes."

Jack started off across the fields at a swift pace, while Mark strolled on down the road, in the direction of the old Preakness house. He was thinking of many things, chiefly of the wonderful journey that lay before them, and he was wondering what the moon would look like when they got to it.

That it would be a wild, desolate place, he had no doubt, for the evidences of the telescopes of astronomers pointed that way, and, as is well known, the most powerful instruments can now bring the moon to within an apparent distance of one hundred miles of the earth. This is true of the Lick telescope, which has a magnifying power of 2,500 and an object lens a yard across.

But, with this powerful telescope, it has been impossible to distinguish any such objects as forests, cities, or any evidences of life on the moon—that is, on the side that has always been turned toward us.

Almost unconsciously, Mark went on faster than he

intended, and, before he knew it, he had arrived at the barn where he had promised to wait for his chum. Mark looked at his watch, and found that he would still have some time to linger before he could expect Jack to return. He sat down on a stone beside the fence, and looked about him. The day was warm for fall, and the last of the crickets were chirping away, while, in distant fields, men could be seen husking corn, or drawing in loads of yellow pumpkins.

"I wonder if we'll have pumpkin pie on the moon," thought Mark. "Though, of course, we won't. I guess all we'll have to eat will be what Washington takes along in the projectile—that is, unless we find people on the other side of the place."

He sat on the stone for some minutes longer, and then, tiring of the inactivity, he arose and strolled about. Something seemed to draw him in the direction of the old house, which he knew was just around the bend in the road.

"I guess there wouldn't be any harm in my going along and taking a peep at it," mused the lad. "It will be some time before Jack returns, and I may be able to catch a glimpse of our man. I think I'll go up where I can see the place, and I can come back in time to meet Jack. I'll do it. Maybe the fellow might escape while I'm waiting."

Mark thus tried to justify himself for his action in not keeping to his agreement with his chum. Of course it was not an important matter, Mark thought, though the results of his simple action were destined to be more far-reaching than he imagined. He thought he would be back in time to meet Jack, and so he strolled on, going more cautiously now, for, in a few minutes he would come in sight of the old, deserted house, and he did not know what he might find there.

Mark's first sight of the Preakness homestead was of two old stone posts, that had once formed a fine gateway. The posts were in ruins, now, and half fallen down, being covered with Virginia creeper, the leaves of which were now a vivid red, mingled with green.

"Nothing very alarming there," said Mark, half aloud. He could just catch a glimpse of the roof of the house over the tops of the trees, which had not yet shed all their leaves. "Guess I'll go on a little farther. Maybe our friend, the enemy, is sitting on the front porch, sunning himself."

Past the old gateway Mark continued, intending to proceed along the highway until he got directly in front of the old mansion. There, he knew, he would have a good view, unobstructed by trees or shrubbery.

When the lad got to this place in the road, he paused, and stooped over, as if tying the lace of his shoe, for it was his intention to pass himself off, if possible, as a casual passerby, so that in case the mysterious man should be in the house, his suspicions would not be aroused by seeing the youth to whom he had written the note staring in at him.

And, while he was apparently fussing with his shoe, Mark was narrowly eying the old house.

"Not a very inviting place," thought Mark. "I don't see why any man who could afford anything better, would stay there —unless he has some strong motive for lingering in this section. And that's probably what this fellow has, and I'd like to discover it. Well, I don't see any signs of him, so I guess I might as well go back, and wait for Jack. He'll be along soon."

He stood up, took a good look at the house, and was about to retrace his steps down the highway, when he saw the sagging front door of the old mansion slowly open. It creaked on the rusty hinges, and Mark stared with all his might as he saw a man emerge, a man who did not look like a tramp, for his clothes were of good material and cut, and fit him well. Nor did he wear a stubbly growth of beard, but, on the contrary, his face was clean shaven. The man was about Mark's size, perhaps a little taller, and nearly as stout. He stood on the sagging porch, and gazed off toward the road.

"Well, if that's the man Dick Johnson got the note from he's changed mightily in appearance," thought Mark, as he looked at the fellow. "He isn't very tall, and he hasn't any black mustache. But of course he may have shaved that off, and I suppose in the dark, and when one is in a hurry to earn a quarter, it's hard to say whether a man is tall or short. I wonder if this can be the person we're looking for?"

Mark hardly knew what to do. He stood in the road, undecided, and fairly stared at the man, who had left the porch, and was walking down the weed-grown path. He was looking straight at Mark, but if the stranger was the person who had written the note, and if he recognized the lad, he gave no sign to that effect.

"Good afternoon," said the man, as he paused at the gap in the front wall, where once a gate had been. "Pleasant day, isn't it."

"Ye—yes," stammered Mark, wondering what to say next.

"Live around here?" went on the man.

"Not very far off."

"Ah, then you know this old shack?"

"Well, I don't get over here, very often. Do you live here?" ventured Mark boldly, determining to do some questioning on his own account.

"Me live here?" cried the man, as if indignant "Well, hardly! I was just passing, and, happening to see the old place, and having a fondness for antiques, I stepped in. But it is in bad shape. I should say tramps make it their hangout."

"It has that name," said Mark.

There was a pause for a moment, and the lad was a trifle embarrassed. The man was gazing boldly at him.

"I guess I've made a mistake," thought Mark. "This can't be the man we want. He doesn't live here, and he doesn't look like him. I'd better be getting back to meet Jack."

"Are you engaged at anything in particular?" questioned the man taking a few steps nearer the youth.

"No, I'm not working, but I expect to take a trip, shortly, with some friends of mine," answered Mark.

"Ah, is that so?" and there was polite inquiry in the man's voice. "Are you going far?"

"Quite a distance." Mark wondered what the man would say if he told him he was going to the moon.

"I wonder if you would do me a favor?" went on the man. "As I was passing through this old house I saw, on one of the outer doors, an old-fashioned knocker. I am a collector of antiques, and I would very much like to have that. But I need help in getting it off. I do not intend to steal it, but if it is left here some tramp may destroy it, and that would be too bad. I intend to remove it, and then hunt up the owners of this place, and purchase it from them."

"It will be hard to discover who are the owners," replied Mark, "as the title is in dispute."

"So much the better for me. Will you help me remove the knocker? I will pay you for your time."

Mark hesitated. He did not like the man's manner, and there was a shifty, uneasy look about his eyes. Still he might be all right. But Mark did not like the idea of going into the old house with him alone. It might be safe, and, again, it might not. But the knocker was on an outside door. There could be no harm in helping him, as long as it was outside. The man saw the hesitation in the lad's manner.

"It will not take us long," the stranger said. "I want you to help me pry off the knocker, as I have no screw-driver to remove it. I will pay you well."

As he spoke he came nearer to Mark, and the lad noticed that the man's right hand was held behind his back. This struck Mark as rather suspicious. Suddenly he became aware of a peculiar odor in the air—a sweet, sickish odor. He started back in alarm, all his former suspicions aroused. The man seemed to leap toward him.

"Look out!" suddenly cried the fellow. "Look behind you!"

Involuntarily Mark turned. He saw nothing alarming. The next instant he felt himself grasped in the strong arms of the man, and a cloth that smelled strongly of the strange, sweetly sickish odor was pressed over the lad's face.

"Here! Stop! Let me go! Help! Help!" cried Mark. Then his

voice died out. He felt weak and sick, and sank back, an inert mass in the man's arms.

"I guess I've got you this time," whispered the fellow, as he gazed down on Mark's white face. "I'll put you where you won't get away, either," and, picking up the youth, he carried him a prisoner into the deserted house.

CHAPTER VIII

JACK IS PUZZLED

Whistling merrily, with his mind as much on the big field of diamonds he expected to discover on the moon, as it was on anything else, Jack Darrow crossed over the meadows toward the telegraph office.

"By Jinks! It certainly will be great to fly through space once more," he mused. "Of course it isn't much of a trip, only a quarter of a million miles at most, but it will be a little outing for us, and then those diamonds!"

A trip of a quarter of a million miles only a little outing! But then what can be expected of lads who had gone to Mars and back again?

Jack lost no time in reaching the telegraph office, where he left the message to be sent, urging the operator to "rush" it, which that official promised to do.

"'Twon't be no great hardship on me, neither," he said with a cheerful grin, "seein' as how this is the only one I've had to send to-day. I'll get it right off for you, Jack."

Jack meant to hurry back, but, just as he was turning out of the main village street, to cut across lots, and join Mark at the place agreed upon, Jack saw two dogs fighting. It was with the best intentions in the world that he ran toward them, for he wanted to separate them. However a man was ahead of him, and soon had the two beasts apart. But Jack lingered several moments to see if there would be a renewal of the hostilities. There wasn't, and he hurried on. In a short time he was within sight of the barn, where his chum had agreed to meet him.

"Mark!" cried Jack, when he came within hailing distance.

There was no response.

"Maybe he's hiding to fool me," thought the lad, "I'll give him another call."

Neither was there a reply to this shout, and Jack, with a vague feeling of fear in his heart, hurried forward, climbed the fence that separated the field from the highway, and fairly ran toward the barn.

A glance sufficed to show that Mark was not in sight, and, thinking that his chum might be on the other side, Jack went around the structure.

"Oh, you Mark!" he called. "I'm back! Let's get a move on and go to the old house."

Silence was the only answer.

"That's queer," murmured Jack, when he had made a circuit of the place, and had seen no sight of his friend. "I wonder if anything could have happened to him? Perhaps he went inside, and has fallen down the hay mow. I'll take a look."

He made a thorough inspection of the ramshackle old structure, but there was no evidence that Mark had entered it, and Jack was soon quite assured that no harm had befallen his friend in there. Then a sudden thought came to him.

"Why, of course!" he exclaimed aloud. "I should have thought of that before. Mark got tired of waiting, and went on to the Preakness house. I might have known. I'll go on and catch up to him there."

Jack had reasoned correctly, but he could not know, what had taken place with only the old, grim, deserted mansion for a witness. With a lighter heart he set off down the road.

It did not take him long, at the pace he kept up, to come within sight of the old gateway, with the creeper twining over the pillars. Then he caught a glimpse of the house, and he at once slackened his footsteps.

"No use rushing into this thing," he reasoned in a whisper. "Mark may be in hiding, taking an observation of the mysterious man, and I don't want to spoil it, by butting in. Guess I'll lie low for a while, and see what develops."

Crouching down beside some bushes that lined the roadway Jack looked toward the silent, tumbled-down house and waited. All was still. Occasionally a shutter flapped in the wind, the hinges creaking dismally, or some of the loose window-panes rattled as the sash was blown to and fro. It was not a pleasant aspect, and as the afternoon was waning, and the sun was going down, while a cool wind sprang up, Jack was anything but comfortable in his place of observation.

And the one objection to it was that there was nothing to observe. Not a sign of life was to be seen about the place, and the broken windows, like so many unblinking eyes, stared out on the fields and road.

"Oh pshaw!" exclaimed Jack at length, "I'm not going to sit here this way! I'm going up and take a look. It can't bite me, and if that man's in there I can give him some sort of a talk that will make it look all right. I'm going closer. Maybe Mark's inside there, waiting for me, though it's queer why he didn't keep his agreement and wait for me at the barn. Well, here goes."

Though he spoke bravely, it was not without a little feeling of apprehension that Jack started toward the old mansion. He kept a close watch for the advent of any person or persons who might be in the house, but, when he reached the front porch, and had seen no one, he felt more at ease.

"Hello, Mark!" he cried boldly. "Are you inside?"

He paused for an answer. None came.

"This is getting rather strange," murmured Jack, who was now quite puzzled as to what to make of the whole matter. "Mark must be here, yet why doesn't he answer me? Oh, you Mark!" he shouted at the top of his voice.

There was only silence, and, after waiting a few moments Jack made up his mind that the best plan would be to enter the house and look around.

He made a hasty search through the lower rooms, but saw no sign of Mark. It was the same upstairs, and on the third floor there was no evidence of his chum. Jack called again, but got no reply.

"The garret next, and then the cellar," he told himself, and these two places, darker and more dismal than any other parts of the old mansion, were soon explored.

"Well, if Mark came here he's not here now," thought Jack, "and there's no use in my staying any longer. Maybe something happened that he had to go back home. Perhaps he's trailing the man. We should have made up some plan to be followed in case anything like that happened."

Deciding that the best thing he could do would be to go back home Jack came out of the old house. As he did so he gave a final call:

"Mark! Oh, you Mark! Are you anywhere about?"

What was that? Was it an answer, or merely the echo of his own voice? Jack started, and then, as he heard another sound, he said:

"Only the wind squeaking a shutter. Mark isn't here."

If Jack had only known!

Through the quickly-gathering darkness Jack turned his steps toward home. On the way along the country road he kept a sharp lookout for any sign of his chum, and, also, he looked to see if he could catch a glimpse of any person who might answer the description of the man they suspected of tampering with the Cardite motor.

But the road was deserted, save for an occasional farmer urging his horses along, that be might the more quickly get home to supper.

"It's mighty strange," mused Jack, as he kept on. "I don't think Mark did just right, and yet, perhaps, when it's all explained, he may have good reasons for what he did. Maybe I'm wrong to worry about him, and, just as likely as not, he's safe home, wondering what kept me. But he might have known that I'd come back to the barn where I said I'd meet him. Of course that dog-fight delayed me a little, but not much."

It was quite dark when Jack reached the house where he and his chum lived with the two professors. There was a cheerful light glowing from many windows, and Jack also noticed an illumination in the shed where the projectile was housed.

"Guess they're working on it, to get it in shape for the trip, sooner than they expected," he mused.

Jack was met at the door by Washington White.

"Hello, Wash!" greeted the lad.

"Good land a' massy! Where hab yo' been transmigatorying yo'se'f during de period when the conglomeration of carbo-hydrates and protoids hab been projected on to de inter-planetary plane ob de rectangle?"

"Do you mean where have I been while supper was getting ready?" asked Jack.

"Dat's 'zackly what I means, Massa Jack."

"Then why don't you say it?"

"I done did. Dat's what I done. Supper's cold. But where am Massa Mark?"

"What! Isn't Mark home?" cried Jack, starting back in alarm.

"No, Massa Jack, we ain't seed him sence yo' two went off togedder. Where yo' all been?"

"Mark not home!" gasped Mark. "Where is Professor Henderson, Wash? I must speak to him at once."

"He am out in de shed wif Massa Roumann."

With fear in his heart Jack dashed out toward the big shed.

"Ain't yo' goin' t' hab some supper?" called Washington.

"I don't want any supper—yet," flung back Jack over his shoulder.

CHAPTER IX

A DARING PLOT

Mark Sampson lay an inert mass in the arms of the man who had attacked him. Through the sagging door of the old, deserted house the captive lad was carried, and up creaking stairs.

"I guess no one saw me," whispered the man. "I'm safe, so far, and I can work my scheme to perfection. Everything turned out well for me. I was just wondering how I could get this youth in my power, and he fairly walked into my hands! Now to keep him safe until I can take his place in the projectile, and have my revenge. I have waited a long time for it, but it has come at last!"

Pausing at the head of the creaking stairs the man looked behind him, to make sure that he was not being followed, but not a sound broke the stillness of the old house, save the rattle and bang of the ruined shutters.

"I'm safe! Safe!" exulted the man, with a cruel chuckle. "Now to bind him, and hide him in the secret chamber."

He laid Mark down on a pile of bagging in a corner of a room at the head of the stairs. Then, still glancing behind him, as if fearful of being observed, the man walked over to a mantlepiece, fumbled about a bit of carving that adorned the centre, and pressed on a certain spot. A moment later the mantle seemed to swing out, and there was revealed a secret room, the existence of which would never have been suspected by the casual observer.

Taking some of the bags from the pile where the unconscious lad was, the man made a rude bed in the secret room. Then he carried Mark in, and placed him in a fairly comfortable position, first taking the precaution, however, of binding his hands and feet.

"There," whispered the man, when he had finished, "I guess you'll not get away in a hurry. Now I'll wait until dark, and then I'll give you something to eat, for I don't want you to starve. But I must keep in hiding, for, very likely, there'll be a search made for him. Guess I'd better stay here, and see what happens," and the mysterious man pressed the spring that sent the mantle back into place again, hiding all traces of the secret room.

"It's a good thing I stumbled upon this hiding place," he said to himself. "It couldn't be better for what I want. Now to see what happens next."

He did not have long to wait, for in a short time Jack, as we have seen, appeared on the scene, and began his search. At the sound of his voice, calling for Mark, the man started in his hiding place, and glanced uneasily at Mark.

"He may hear, and wake up," he whispered.

Jack came upstairs in the deserted house, and continued his search there, calling from time to time. He gave one loud shout at the head of the stairs, and the very thing that the man feared would happen came to pass.

The effect of the drug having worn off, Mark stirred uneasily, and started up. He heard Jack's cry, and uttered a half-articulate answer. In an instant the man was at his side, and had quickly gagged him. This had the further effect of awakening the unfortunate lad; and he struggled to loosen his bonds, but they were too strongly tied. He endeavored to answer Jack, but only a meaningless mumble resulted, for the gag was effective.

"All you have to do is to keep quiet," urged the man, as he knelt beside Mark in the darkness. "As soon as your chum goes, I'll take that thing out of your mouth, and give you something to eat."

Jack's voice died away, and presently, as the ears of the man told him, the boy left the old house. Waiting some time, to make sure that he would not return, the man removed the knot of rags from Mark's mouth, and slightly loosened his bonds, first warning him, however, that if he attempted to escape he would be harshly dealt with.

"But what right have you to keep me here?" demanded the youth. "Who are you, and what have I done to you, that you should treat me this way? Are you crazy? Don't you know that you are liable to arrest for this?"

"No one can arrest me," boasted the fellow.

"But why have you made me a prisoner?" demanded Mark.

"For reasons of my own. You'll see very soon."

"But what have I done to you?" persisted the lad. "I never saw you before, that I know of, unless you are the man who sent me the note, and who ran when my chum and I came to the bridge to meet you."

"I'm the man," was the answer, with a chuckle.

"Then you must be the one who tried to wreck our projectile," went on Mark.

"Yes, I did that, and now I am sorry for it, for I have thought of a much better scheme for getting even, and having my revenge on you."

"But why do you want to be revenged on us?"

"Because of what you have done!" and the man's voice took on an ugly tone.

"But what did we do?" begged Mark.

"You'll know soon enough," was the answer, with a cunning laugh, and then Mark was sure he had to deal with a lunatic. He ceased his struggles to loosen the bonds, and resolved to meet cunning with cunning. He would bide his time.

"Will you promise to be quiet, and not kick up a fuss if I get you something to eat?" asked the man.

"Yes; but I'd rather have a drink of water first. I feel sick."

"Very well, you shall have some water. I'll have to go out and get it, but I must first blindfold you, so that you will not discover the secret of this room."

Mark could not help himself, for he was bound, and when the man had tied a handkerchief over his eyes, Mark heard his captor moving about.

Next there came a sound as of some heavy body, or object, being pushed across the room. Mark felt a draught of wind on his face, but it ceased instantly, and he knew that he was alone. He tried to work the bandage from over his eyes, and he endeavored to loosen his bonds, for he did not consider that this violated his promise. But it was of no effect.

Presently he heard the moving, shoving sound again, and once more felt the wind on his face. Then he heard the voice of his captor speaking.

"Here is food and drink. I'm going to untie your hands so you can eat, but mind, no fighting, for I'm a desperate man, and I won't stand any nonsense!"

He fumbled about the bonds, and soon Mark was free to stand up and use his hands. The bandage was taken from his eyes, and he was able to peer about his prison by the light of a candle which his captor had brought.

Mark's first glance was at the man. He was the same one who had emerged from the house to attack and drug him, but as for recognizing in him the person who had been at the bridge, this was impossible. As far as Mark could tell he had never seen the man before, nor did he answer the description given by Dick Johnson.

There was little danger that Mark would attempt violence. He was too weak, and his jailer seemed a powerful fellow. Then, too, the lad felt ill from the effects of the drug.

"Drink some water, and eat a bit, and you'll feel better," urged the man, which advice Mark followed, though, his appetite was not of the best, and he was much worried as to what his friends would think about his strange disappearance.

"What do you intend to do with me?" asked Mark, when he felt a little better from the effects of the food and drink. The man had sat on an old soap box, and watched his captive while he ate.

"Do with you? Why, I'm going to keep you here until your friends have left in the projectile," was the answer.

"But why don't you want me to go with them?"

"Oh, I have my reasons. You'll find out soon enough. You can't go, that's all."

"But why do you take such an interest in me? Why didn't you capture my chum Jack, too, while you were about it?"

"Two reasons. One was that Jack wouldn't answer my purpose, and the other was that I didn't have a chance to get him. You walked right into my trap, just when I was doing my best to think of another plan to get hold of you, since my first one failed."

"But what is your purpose?" insisted the lad. "What do you want with me?" He thought perhaps if he questioned the man closely enough he might discover something that would give him a clew, or might aid him to escape.

"You'll learn soon enough," was the answer.

"Will you tell me your name?" asked Marie quietly.

"No—why should I?" was the quick reply. "If I told you who I was you would at once know why I have made you a captive here. No; you shall hear all in good time, but that will not be until I am ready.

"Now," went on his captor, after a period of silence, "I shall have to bind and blindfold you again."

"Why?" asked Mark, in some alarm.

"Because I don't want you to see how I get in and out of this room, and that's the only way I can guard my secret. Though if you promise not to remove the bandage from your eyes within five minutes from the time I leave you, I will not have to tie your hands and feet. After I am gone you may take the handkerchief off, but when you hear me rap on the wall, ready to come back again, you must once more blindfold yourself. Otherwise I shall have to tie you up."

Mark considered a moment. It was not pleasant to be tied with the cruel ropes, and he felt that in time he could penetrate the mystery of how the room opened, even if he did not see his jailer enter and leave.

"I promise," he said finally.

"That's good. It simplifies matters. Now you can blindfold yourself, and I trust to your honor. You may remove the bandage in five minutes, but when you hear me knock, you must replace it until I am in the apartment. Then you can take it off again."

There was little choice but to obey, and Mark tied the handkerchief over his eyes. He listened intently, heard the man moving about the room, felt the wind on his cheeks, and then came silence.

He waited until he thought five minutes had passed, and then took off the bandage. The candle was burning where the man had set it, but the fellow himself was gone. He had taken with him the broken dishes, and remains of the food Mark had not eaten. The glass and a pitcher of water stood on a broken table, and Mark took a big drink.

"Now to see if I can't get out of this place," he murmured to himself.

Mark had invented many pieces of apparatus, and he was considered a good mechanician. Consequently he went about his task in a systematic manner. He examined the walls carefully by the candle, which he carried in his hand, but no opening was apparent.

"Of course, there must be some secret spring to press," said the lad. "That's how he gets in and out. A section of the wall moves, but where it is I can't see. It will take time. I must look at every inch."

He was in the midst of his investigations when there sounded on the wall back of him three raps.

"Ha! At least, that tells me where the opening is," thought the lad. "It's on that side, but now I have to put that blamed bandage on. Well, I may be able to escape yet."

True to his promise, he blindfolded himself well, and presently he heard a noise, felt a draught of air, and he knew his captor was in the room.

"You can now take off the handkerchief," said the man. "I have brought you some more bags for bed clothing. It isn't much, but it is all I have. They will keep you warm tonight."

"Are you going to imprison me over night?" asked Mark.

"Yes, and I'll stay here with you. No one can find us here. The secret room is well hidden. But first I have another matter that needs attention. I am going to ask you a question."

"What?" asked the captive, wondering what strange request the mentally unbalanced man would make now.

The man leaned forward and whispered something in Mark's ear, as if he was afraid the very walls would hear.

"I'll not do it!" cried the youth. "I'll never aid you to deceive my friends, for that is your object. I'll never do it!"

"Then I shall have to use force," was the determined response. "You may take your choice!"

Poor Mark did not know what to do, yet there was little he could choose between. The man had him in his power, yet the lad was terribly afraid of the result of the daring scheme which he knew was in the mind of the lunatic, for such he believed the man to be.

"Will you not give up this plan?" begged Mark. "I know Professor Henderson will pay you any sum in reason to let me go. You can become a rich man."

"I don't want riches—I want revenge!" exclaimed the man. And he glared at Mark, while throughout the dismal, deserted house there sounded the rattle and bang of the flapping shutters.

CHAPTER X

MARK'S STRANGE ACTIONS

Jack Darrow fairly burst into the big shed where the two scientists were at work over the ruined motor. They looked up at his excitable entrance, and Mr. Henderson called out:

"Why, Jack, what's the matter?"

"Quite a lot, I'm afraid," answered the lad, and there was that in his voice which alarmed the professors.

"What do you mean?" inquired Mr. Roumann, laying aside some of the damaged motor plates.

"Mark's gone!" gasped Jack.

"Gone! Where?" exclaimed Mr. Henderson.

"I don't know, but he went to the deserted house, where we thought the mysterious man was hiding, and since then I can't find him."

Then the frightened lad proceeded to explain what he and Mark had undertaken, and the outcome of it; how his chum had failed to meet him at the rendezvous, and how Jack had searched through the old house without result.

"There's but one thing to do," declared Professor Henderson, when he had listened to the story. "We must go back there and make a more thorough search."

"What—to-night?" exclaimed the German.

"Surely. Why not? We can't leave Mark there all alone. He may be hurt, or in trouble."

"That's what I think," said Jack. "I'll tell Washington and Andy, and we'll go back and hunt for him. Poor Mark! If he had only waited for me, perhaps this would never have happened, and if I hadn't stopped at the dog-fight maybe Mark would have waited for me. Well, it's too late to worry about that now. The thing is to find him; and I guess we can."

Jack would not stop longer than to snatch a hasty bite of supper before he joined the searching party. Washington and he carried lanterns, while Andy Sudds had his trusty rifle, and the two professors brought up in the rear, armed with stout clubs, for Jack's account of the affair made them think that perhaps they might have to deal with a violent man.

"Hadn't you better notify the police?" suggested Andy. "A couple of constables would be some help."

"Not very much," declared Jack. "Besides, there are only two in Bayside, and it's hard to locate either one when you want them. I guess we can manage alone."

"Yes, I would rather not notify the police if it can be avoided," said Professor Henderson.

The searching party hurried along the country highway, which was now deserted, as it was quite dark. Their lanterns flashed from side to side, but they had no hope of getting any trace of Mark until they came to the old barn, at least, though Jack wished several times that he might meet his chum running toward them along the road.

They reached the barn in due course, and while Washington, Jack and Andy began a search of it, the two scientists went up to the house of the man who owned it and enlisted his aid. They asked him if he had seen Mark around that afternoon, but the farmer had not.

"But me an' my hired man'll come out and help you hunt through the barn," he said. "I remember once, when I was a lad, that my brother fell off the hay mow and lay unconscious in a manger for five hours before we found him. Maybe that's what's happened to this young man," suggested Mr. Hampton, which was the farmer's name.

"I looked around pretty well this afternoon," explained Jack, when the farmer and his man had reached the barn, "but, of course, I didn't know all the nooks and corners."

A thorough search of the structure, however, failed to reveal the presence of Mark, and then the farmer volunteered to accompany the party on to the old Preakness house. His offer was received with thanks, and, bringing two more lanterns with them, Mr. Hampton and his man added considerable to the illumination.

They went through the old mansion from garret to cellar, and called repeatedly, but there was no answer. And good reason, for in the secret room, with his captive, the mysterious man heard the first approach of the searching party; and he quickly bound Mark and gagged him, so that he could not answer.

There was nothing to do but to leave, and it was with sad hearts that Jack and his friends departed, their search having been unavailing. They turned toward home, which they reached quite late, but found nothing disturbed.

No one in Professor Henderson's house slept much that night, and in the morning pale and wan faces looked at each other, all asking the same question: "Where is Mark?"

But no one could answer.

They talked over the matter, and decided that Jack, with Andy and Washington, should form a searching party to scour the surrounding country. The two scientists were too old for such work, and, as the aid of the police was not desired, it was felt that the three could do all that was necessary.

Accordingly, while Professor Henderson and his German friend went to work on the damaged motor, which did not need as much repairing as at first was thought to put it in working shape again, Jack and the two men started off to hunt for Mark.

They were gone all that day, returning very much discouraged at dusk, saying that they could get no trace of him.

"I don't see where he can be!" exclaimed Jack desperately, for, though the two lads were not related, they had been friends so long, and had shared so many pleasures and dangers together, that they were like brothers. "You won't start for the moon until you find him, will you, Professor?" asked Jack.

"No, indeed; though we could start to-morrow if he was here," replied the aged scientist. "The special tools came to-day, and the motor has been repaired. We have tested it, and the Cardite power works even better than did the Etherium apparatus."

"Then we can start as soon as Mark is found?" asked Andy Sudds.

"Yes, for everything has been put inside the projectile, and all that remains is to haul it out of the shed, point it at the moon, and start the motor."

"Then I guess I'll give my gun a final cleaning, and get ready. There may be good hunting on the moon," said the old hunter.

Jack was tired from his long tramp that day, searching for his missing chum, but before he went to bed he wanted to go out and take a look at the big projectile, which was now ready to start for the moon.

As he turned around the corner of the immense shed to enter the door, he was startled by seeing a figure coming toward him. Jack started, rubbed his eyes, and peered again.

"Is it possible? Can I be mistaken?" he whispered.

The figure came nearer. Jack, who had come to a halt, broke into a run.

"Mark! Mark!" he cried joyously. "Oh, you've come back! Where have you been?"

Jack was about to clasp his chum in his arms when he saw that Mark's arm was in a sling, and that his face was all bandaged up, so that scarcely any of his features showed. Had it not been for the clothes, and a certain stoutness of which Mark never could seem to get rid, Jack would scarcely have known his friend.

"Why, Mark, what happened?" cried Jack. "Have you met with an accident? Where have you been? In a hospital? What became of you? Why didn't you wait for me?"

"I can't answer all those questions at once," was the reply, and Jack thought Mark's voice was curiously muffled and hoarse, entirely unlike his usual tones. But he ascribed that to the bandages around the mouth.

"Well, answer one at a time then," said Jack, and there was an undefinable, strange air about his chum which cooled Jack's first impulse of gladness. "Whatever happened to you, Mark? Are you hurt?"

"I was—yes," came the reply, in short, jerky tones. "I had an accident, and I've been in a hospital. That's why I couldn't send you word. But I'm all right now. When does the projectile start?"

"To-morrow, now that you're here. But tell me more about it. Where were you hurt?"

"On my head and arm."

"No; I mean where did the accident occur?"

"Oh, in the old house where I went to—to look for that man."

"Did you find him?" asked Jack eagerly.

"No. He's not there now."

"Well, never mind. We won't bother about him. Come on to the house. My, but I'm glad to see you again! And so will the others be."

In his enthusiasm at seeing his chum again Jack wanted to hug him. He approached Mark, but the latter cried out:

"Look out! Don't come too close!"

"Why not? Have you caught some disease?"

"No, but you might hurt my broken arm!"

"Oh, is it broken? That's tough luck. Did you fall?"

"Yes—in the old house. I fell down stairs."

"And your head is all bandaged up, too," went on Jack, trying to peer into his friend's face through the roll of bandages.

"Look out! Don't come too near!" again warned the other. "You might jostle against me, and knock off some of the bandages."

"Did you lose some of your teeth, the reason your voice sounds so funny?" asked Jack.

"Yes, I did knock out a few when I tumbled. But don't bother about me. I'll be all right soon. Let's go in the house. I want to go to bed."

"But they'll all want to see you, and hear about the accident, Mark," insisted Jack. "My, but we've been all worked up about you. How did you happen to be taken to a hospital?"

"A farmer came along, and I hailed him. Then I lost

consciousness, and couldn't let you know where I was. But never mind the details. I'm anxious to get started on the trip to the moon. Couldn't we start to-night?"

"I don't believe so. You need rest. But come on in the house." Then Jack hurried on ahead, calling: "Mark's found! Mark is back!"

His cries brought all of the others out on the porch, and at first they could scarcely believe the good news, but soon Jack and the new arrival came in sight. As Jack had been, the two professors and the others were startled when they saw how Mark was bundled up in bandages.

"He fell down stairs," explained Jack.

"Come over here where it's light, so I can see you," suggested Professor Henderson. "Perhaps some of the bandages have slipped off since you came from the hospital. Why did you come alone? Why didn't you send us word where you were as soon as you were conscious, and we would have come for you."

"Oh, I didn't want to bother you," explained the bundled-up figure. "I managed to walk it all right."

"But your injuries may need attention," insisted Mr. Henderson. "I know something about doctoring. Come here where I can see."

"No—no—the—light hurts my eyes," was the hasty reply. "I guess I'll go to bed, so as to be all ready to start in the morning. Why don't you leave for the moon to-night, professor?"

"There are still a few little details to look after. But are you sure you are well enough to go with us? We may meet with hardships up on the moon."

"Oh, I'm all ready to go," was the answer. "I'd start to-night if I could. But now I must get to bed."

"Don't you want supper?" asked Jack.

"No, I had some just before I left the hospital."

"What hospital was it?" inquired Andy Sudds. "I was in one once, and I didn't like it. There wa'nt enough air for me."

"I forget the name of the place," came the reply. "I can't think clearly. I need sleep."

The newcomer kept in the shadows of the room, as if the light hurt his eyes, and appeared restless and ill at ease. With the hand that was not in a sling he pulled the bandages closer about his face.

"Can't you tell us more about what happened?" asked Jack, for Mark was not usually so reticent, and his chum noticed it.

"There isn't much to tell," was the response. "I went to the old house, and I was looking around when I happened to tumble down stairs. I must have been knocked unconscious, but when I came to I crawled outside. A farmer was driving past, and I asked him to take me to a hospital."

"Why didn't you come home?" asked Mr. Henderson.

"Oh, I didn't want to make any trouble and delay work on the projectile. I figured that I could be with you in a few hours, and you wouldn't worry. But they insisted that I must stay in the hospital when they got me there. Then I lost consciousness again, and couldn't manage to let you know where I was. But I'm all right now."

"Why didn't you wait for me at the barn, when I went to send the telegram, as you promised you would?" asked Jack, who felt a little hurt at his chum's neglect.

"Did I promise to wait for you at some barn?"

"Yes; don't you remember?" and Jack gazed at the bandaged figure in surprise.

"Oh, yes—I—I guess I do. But I want to go to bed now," and pulling the cloths closer about his face the injured one started from the apartment.

"Here. That's not the way up to your room. The stairs are over here," called Jack, for he saw the newcomer taking the wrong direction.

"Oh, yes. Guess my mind must be wandering," and with an uneasy laugh the injured one turned about. They heard him going up stairs, and a little later Jack followed. He found that Mark's room was not occupied.

"Hi, Mark! Where are you?" he called, in some alarm.

"Here," was the answer, and the voice came from Jack's own apartment.

"Well, you're in the wrong bunk."

"Am I? Well, I must have made another mistake. My head can't be right," and with that the other came out and hastily went into the adjoining apartment.

For a moment Jack stood in the hall. He looked at the door that had closed behind the bandaged figure.

"There's something wrong," said Jack in a low voice. "How strange Mark acts! I wonder what can be the matter?"

CHAPTER XI

READY FOR THE MOON

There were busy times for the moon-voyagers the next day. They were up early, for at the last moment many little details needed to be settled. The Cardite motor had been thoroughly repaired, for the damage caused by the unknown enemy had done no permanent harm.

When the injured one appeared the bandage on his head seemed larger than ever, and his features were almost hidden. He still wore his arm in a sling.

"Well, how do you feel?" asked Jack, looking narrowly at the figure. He could not get rid of a suspicion that something was wrong with Mark.

"Oh, I'm feeling pretty fair," was the mumbled answer. "I didn't sleep much, though."

"Well, take care of yourself," advised Jack. "We are about ready to start. We'll get off about noon, Professor Henderson says. Don't try to do anything and injure your broken arm. You certainly had a tough time of it."

"Yes, I guess I did. I can't do much to help you."

"You don't need to. We're all but finished. Just hang around and watch me work. There isn't much to do."

But though Jack gave an invitation to remain near him, the other seemed to prefer being off by himself. He wandered in and out of the projectile, now and then helping Andy or Washington to carry light objects into the *Annihilator*. But all the while he was careful not to disturb the bandage on his face, and several times he stopped to readjust it. Nor did he talk much, which Jack ascribed to his statement that his teeth hurt him. And when the bandaged figure did speak, it was in mumbling tones, very different from Mark's usually cheerful ones.

"Well," remarked Professor Roumann, after a final inspection of the big Cardite motor—the one that was to be depended on to carry them to the moon—"I think we are about ready to leave this earth. How about it, Professor Henderson?"

"Yes, I think so. Have you made any calculation as to speed?"

"Yes, we will not have to move nearly as fast as we did when we went to Mars. We only have to cover a quarter of a million of miles at the most, and probably less than that. The motor will send us along at the rate of about a mile a second, which is three thousand six hundred miles an hour, or eighty-six thousand four hundred miles a—day. At that rate we would be at the moon in less than three days.

"But I don't want to travel as fast as that," the German went on. "I want time to make some scientific observations on the way, and so I have reduced the speed of the Cardite motor by half, though should we need to hasten our trip we can do so."

"Then we'll be about a week on the way?" asked Jack.

"About that, yes," assented Mr. Roumann.

"And could we go farther than to the moon if we wanted to?" inquired the bandaged figure mumblingly.

"Farther? What do you mean?" asked Professor Henderson quickly.

"I mean could we go to Mars if we wanted to?"

"You don't mean to say you want to go back there, and run the chance of being attacked by the savage Martians, do you?" asked Jack.

"No, I was only asking," and the other seemed confused.

"Well, of course, we *could* go there, as we have plenty of supplies and enough of the Cardite," said Mr. Roumann. "But I think the moon will be the limit of our trip this time."

The work went on, the last things to be put aboard the projectile being a number of scientific instruments. The injured one wandered in and out, now being in the house and again in the big shed. He seemed restless and ill at ease, and frequently he walked to the front gate and gazed down the road.

"You seem to be looking for some one," spoke Jack. "Are you expecting your girl to come along and bid you good-by, Mark?"

"Who—me? No, I—I was just looking to see if—if it was going to rain."

"Rain? Well, rain won't make much difference to us soon. We will be outside of the earth's atmosphere in a jiffy after we have started, and then rain won't worry us. Is your stateroom all fixed up?"

"No, I didn't think of that. Guess I'd better look after it."

The two started together for the projectile. The stout one entered first, and made his way through the engine room and main cabin to the compartment off which the staterooms opened. He entered one.

"Here, that's not yours," cried Jack. "That's where Professor Henderson sleeps. Yours is next to mine."

"That's right; I forgot," mumbled the other. "I must be getting absent minded since my accident. But I'll be all right soon. I'll get my room to rights, and then probably we'll start."

"I guess so," answered Jack, but he shook his head as he gazed after his chum. "Mark has certainly changed," he murmured. "I wish he'd take those bandages off, so I could get a look at his face."

The last details were completed. The big *Annihilator* had been run out on trucks into the yard surrounding the shed, ready to be hurled through the air. The shop, shed and house had been locked up and given in charge of a caretaker, who would remain on guard until our friends returned.

"Are we all ready?" asked Professor Henderson, as he stood ready to close the main entrance door and seal it hermetically.

"All ready, I guess," answered Jack. The stout one had gone

to his stateroom, where he could be heard moving about.

"I'm ready," announced Professor Roumann. "Say the word and I'll start the motor." He was in the engine room, looking over the machinery. At that moment there came a loud yell from the galley where Washington White was.

"Heah, heah! Come back!" cried the colored man. "My Shanghai rooster is got loose!" he yelled, and, an instant later, the fowl came sailing out of the projectile, with Washington in full chase after him.

"I'll help you catch him," volunteered Jack, springing to the cook's aid, while Professor Henderson laughed, and a bandaged figure, looking from a stateroom port, wondered at the delay in starting the projectile.

CHAPTER XII

MARK'S ESCAPE

Mark Sampson was alone in the deserted house. Bound hand and foot, stripped of his clothing, and attired in some old garments that the tramps who made a hanging-out place of the old mansion had cast aside, the unfortunate lad was stretched on a pile of bagging, his heart beating partly with fear and partly with rage over a desire to escape and punish the scoundrel responsible for his plight.

The man who had captured him, after taking away Mark's clothes, had chuckled, as though at some joke.

"You may think this is funny," spoke the lad bitterly, "but you won't be so pleased when my friends get after you."

"They'll never get after me," boasted the man. "This is a good joke. To think that I can pass myself off as you; that I can join them in the projectile, and they never will be the wiser!"

"They'll soon discover that you are disguised as me," declared Mark, "and when they do they'll have you arrested."

"Yes, but they'll not discover it until we have left the earth, and are on our way to the moon. Then it will be too late to turn back, and my object will have been accomplished. I will be with them in the *Annihilator*, and I'll have my revenge! The projectile is due to sail to-morrow, and I'll be on hand. I'm going to leave you now. I have left orders with a friend of mine that you are to be released to-morrow night. In the meanwhile you will have to be as comfortable as you can. I wish you no harm, but I must keep you here.

"I will feed you well before I go, and put some water where you can get it. But I must leave you tied. I'll not gag you, for, no matter how you yell, no one will hear you. I have posted a notice in front of this place that it is under the watch of the police, so no tramps will venture in, and your friends will not come back.

"Now, just make yourself comfortable here, and I'll go to the moon in your place. I think I shall enjoy the trip. As I said, you will be released to-morrow night, several hours after the projectile has left the earth."

"How do you know it is to start to-morrow morning?" asked Mark.

"Oh, I have been spying around, and I overheard the professors talking. I know a thing or two, and I'll be on hand, on time, in your place! Now, I have to leave you. I've left ten dollars to pay for your suit, which I need to disguise myself with."

Then the man was gone, and Mark was left with his bitter thoughts to keep him company. The whole daring scheme of the man had been revealed. He did look something like Mark, and, attired in the lad's clothes, and by keeping his face concealed, he might pass himself off as Jack's chum; at least, until after the projectile had started.

"And then, as he says, it will be too late to return to earth and get me," thought Mark bitterly. "Oh, why did I ever try to learn this man's secret? Who is he, anyhow? Why didn't I wait for Jack at the barn, as I promised? It's all my fault. I wonder if I can't get loose?"

Mark struggled several hours desperately and at last he felt the ropes giving slightly. He redoubled his efforts. Strand by strand the cords parted. He put all his efforts into one last attempt, and to his great joy he felt his hands separate. He was partly free!

But scarcely half his task was accomplished. He had yet to discover the secret of the hidden room—a room, as he afterward learned, which had been built during slavery days to conceal the poor black men who were escaping from the South.

"But now I have my hands to work with!" exulted Mark.

Resting a bit after his strenuous labors, he took a long drink of water and attacked the ropes on his feet. They were comparatively easy to loosen, and soon he stood up unbound.

"Now for the secret panel!" he exclaimed, for he was convinced that it was by some such means that his captor had entered and left. As has already been explained, Mark knew on which side of his prison the opening was likely to be—it would be where the warning knocks had sounded. He began a minute inspection of that wall.

But if Mark hoped to speedily discover the secret he was doomed to disappointment. He went over every inch of the surface, seemingly, and pressed on every depression or projection that met his eye, as he passed the candle flame along the wall.

Roy Rockwood

Success did not reward him, and, as hour after hour passed, and the candle burned lower and lower, Mark began to despair.

"I must escape before the projectile leaves," he murmured. "It will never do to let them take that man with them under the impression that they have me. I must escape! I will!"

Once more he began the tiresome task of seeking the secret spring. The candle was spluttering in the socket now. It would burn hardly another minute. Desperately Mark sought.

At last, just as the candle gave a dying gasp and flared brightly up prior to going out, the lad saw a small screw head he had not noticed before. It was sunk deep in a board.

"I'll press that and see what happens!" he exclaimed.

With a suddenness that was startling, he found himself in total darkness. The candle had burned out, but he had his finger on the screw. He pressed it with all his force.

There was a rumbling sound in the darkness, a movement as if some heavy body had slid out of the way, and Mark felt a breath of air on his cheeks. Then he saw a dim light.

"Oh, I'm out! I'm out!" he cried joyously, breathing a prayer of thankfulness at his deliverance. "I'm free! I pushed on the right spring, and the panel slid back!"

He fairly leaped forward. The morning light was streaming in through the broken windows. He saw himself in the old hall of the mansion, at the head of the stairs, in a sort of anteroom, the mantle of which apartment had swung aside to give him egress from the secret chamber through a hole in the wall. He was free!

"But am I in time?" he cried. "It is morning—and about ten o'clock, I should judge. I've been working to get free all night. Will I be in time?"

He gave one last look behind at his prison and sprang down the rickety stairs. He had but one thought—to reach home in time to unmask the villain who was impersonating him—to be in time to make the journey to the moon.

"But it's several miles, and I can't walk very fast," murmured Mark. "I'm too stiff and weak. How can I do it?"

He thought of making his way to the nearest farm house, and asking for the loan of a horse and carriage, but he looked so much like a tramp that no farmer would lend him a horse.

"And I need to make speed," he murmured.

At that moment he heard a noise down the road. It was a steady "chug-chug," like some distant motor-boat, but there was no water near at hand.

"A motorcycle!" exclaimed Mark. "Some one is coming on a motorcycle. Oh, if I could only borrow it!"

He ran down into the road. He could see the rider now. To his joy it was Dick Johnson—the lad who had brought him the mysterious note.

"Hi Dick! Dick! hold on!" cried Mark.

The lad on the motor gave one glance at the ragged figure that had hailed him. Then he turned on more power to escape from what he thought was a savage tramp.

"Wait! Stop! I want that motorcycle!" cried Mark.

"Well, you're not going to get it!" yelled back Dick. "I'll send the police after you."

Mark couldn't understand. Then a glance down at his ragged garments showed him what was the matter.

"Wait! Hold on, Dick!" he cried, running forward. "I'm Mark Sampson! I've had a terrible time! I was captured by that mysterious man, and he's got my clothes. I must get home quick!"

Dick heard, but scarcely understood. However, he comprehended that his friend was in trouble, and he wanted to help him. He slowed up, and Mark reached him.

"Lend me your motorcycle, Dick," begged Mark. "I must get home in a hurry to unmask a scoundrel. I'll leave your machine for you at our house. I won't hurt it. I'm in a hurry! Get off!"

Somewhat dazed, Dick dismounted, and Mark climbed into the saddle. He began to pedal, and then threw in the gasolene and spark. The cycle chugged off.

"I'll leave it for you at our house," Mark called back. "I'm going on a trip to the moon, and I don't want to be late."

He was fast disappearing in a cloud of dust, while Dick, gazing after him, remarked:

"Well, I always thought those fellows were crazy to go off in projectiles and things like that, and now I'm sure of it. Going to the moon! Well, I only hope he doesn't take my motor-cycle there!"

Mark sped on, turning the handle levers to get the last notch of speed out of the cycle. Would he be in time?

CHAPTER XIII

A DIREFUL THREAT

Perhaps Washington White's Shanghai rooster did not care to make the trip to the moon, or perhaps the fowl had not yet seen enough of this earth. At any rate, when he flew from the projectile, uttering loud crows, and landed some distance away, he began to run back toward the coop in the rear of the yard.

"Cotch him, cotch him!" yelled the colored man. "Dat's a valuable bird!"

"We'll get him when he goes in the coop," said Jack, who found it difficult to run and laugh at the same time.

"Shall I fire my rifle off and scare him?" asked Andy Sudds.

"No, you might kill him or scare him t' death," objected Washington.

"Come on, Mark, and help," cried Jack, looking toward the projectile, where a figure was peering from the glass-covered port of the main cabin.

But the figure, whose hand was done up in voluminous

bandages, did not come out, and Jack wondered the more at what he thought was a growing strangeness on the part of his chum.

Jack, followed by Andy and Washington, raced off after the rooster, while the two professors, somewhat amused, rather chaffed at the delay. But afterward they were glad of it.

"Just my luck!" muttered the bandaged one. "This delay comes at the wrong time. Why don't they go on without that confounded rooster? If we stay here too long, that fellow Mark may get loose and spoil the whole thing, or Jenkins may go and release him before the time set. It would be just like Jenkins! I've a good notion to start the projectile myself. I know how to operate the Cardite motor. Only I suppose those two professors are on guard in the engine room. I'll have to wait until they catch that rooster, I guess, but I'd like to wring his neck!"

The chase after the fowl was kept up.

"I've got him now!" cried Jack a little later, as the fowl, evidently now much exhausted, ran into another fence corner, where Jack caught him, and shut him up in the coop in the projectile.

"Yo' suttinly am de mos' contrary-minded specimen ob de chicken fambly dat I eber seed," observed Washington, breathing heavily, for his run had winded him.

"Well, are we all ready to start now?" asked Professor Henderson. "No more live stock loose, is there, Jack?"

"I think not."

"Where's Mark? Wasn't he helping you catch the rooster?"

"No, he's inside. Shall I seal the door?"

"Yes, and I'll tell Professor Roumann that we're about to start. All ready for the moon trip!"

Jack was pulling the steel portal toward him. An eager face, peering from a port, waited anxiously for the tremor which would indicate that the projectile had left the earth. In another moment they would be off.

But what was that sound coming from down the highway. A steady chug-chug—a sort of roar, as of a battery of rapid-fire guns going off in double relays! And, mingled with the explosions, there was a voice shouting:

"Wait! Hold on! Don't go without me! I'm Mark Sampson! Don't start the projectile!"

"Somebody must be in a mighty hurry on a motorcycle," thought Jack, as he paused a moment before fastening the door. Then the shouts came to his ears.

"Mark Sampson!" he cried.

Again came the cry: "Wait! Wait! Don't go without me! You've got that mysterious man on board!"

"Mark Sampson!" murmured Jack again. "That's his voice sure enough! I wonder—can it be possible—that man—with his head all bandaged up—his queer actions—I—I—"

Words failed the youth. Throwing wide open the door, he sprang out of the projectile. A moment later there dashed into the yard, where the great projectile rested, a strange figure astride of a puffing motorcycle. The figure was torn and, ragged, and the nondescript garments were covered with dust, for Mark had had a fall. But there was no mistaking the face that peered eagerly forward.

"Jack!" cried the youth on the machine.

"Mark!" ejaculated the lad who had sprung from the projectile. "What has happened? Who is the fellow who has been masquerading as you?"

"A scoundrel and a villain! Let me get at him!" and, slamming on the brakes, as he shut off the power, Mark leaped from the motorcycle, stood it up against the projectile, and clasped his chum by the hand.

"What's the matter?" asked Professor Henderson, as he, too, ran out of the *Annihilator*. "What does that tramp want, Jack? Give him some money, and get back in here; we ought to have started long ago." He looked at the ragged figure.

"This isn't a tramp," cried Jack. "It's Mark!"

"Mark! I thought—"

"There have been strange doings," gasped the lad in tramp's garments. "I have just escaped from being kept a prisoner. Where is the mysterious man? Oh, I'm glad I arrived in time! Were you about to start?"

"That's what we were," replied Jack. "Oh, Mark, but I'm glad to see you again! I didn't know what to think. You acted so strange—or, rather, the fellow we thought was you had me guessing!"

"Good land a' massy!" exclaimed Washington White, as he stood in the doorway, with Andy Sudds behind him. "Am dere two Marks? What's up, anyhow?"

"Don't let that fellow get away—the fellow who passed himself off as me!" shouted Mark. "Lock him up! There's some mystery about him that must be explained. He's a dangerous man to be at large."

Professor Henderson turned back to enter the projectile. Jack advised Andy to get his gun ready, with which to threaten the scoundrel in case of necessity.

At that instant there sounded a crash of glass, and the whole front of the big observation window in the side of the *Annihilator* was smashed to atoms. A figure leaped—a figure which no longer had its head bandaged, and whose arm was no longer in a sling—the figure of a man— the mysterious man who had held Mark a prisoner!

"There he goes!" shouted Jack. "Catch him, somebody! Andy, where's your gun?"

"I'll have it in a jiffy!" cried the hunter, as he dashed back to get it.

But the man did not linger. Scrambling to his feet after his fall, caused by his leap from the broken window, which he had smashed with a sledge hammer as soon as he understood that his game was up, he raced out of the yard. He turned long enough to shake his fist at the group assembled around the projectile, and then leaped away, calling out some words which they could not hear.

"Let's take after him," proposed Mark.

"Come on," seconded Jack.

"No, let him go; he's a desperate man, and you came just in time to unmask him," said Professor Henderson. "He might harm you if you took after him. Let him go. He has not done much damage. We can easily replace the broken window. But I can't understand what his object was in disguising himself as Mark. He certainly looked like you, Mark, especially when he kept his face concealed. Why did he do it?"

"He wanted to go to the moon in my place," answered the former prisoner of the deserted house.

"But why?" insisted Jack.

"Because, I think, he's crazy, and he didn't really know what he did want. But he certainly had me well concealed," spoke Mark. "I'm free now, however, and as soon as I get some decent clothes on I'll go with you to the moon. I wouldn't want the moon people to see me dressed this way."

"How did it happen?" asked Jack. "Tell us all about it. My! but I certainly have been puzzled since you—or rather since the person we thought was you—came back last night all bunged up. Give us the story."

"I will; give me a chance. I guess that villain is gone for good." Andy Sudds came out with his gun, and insisted on taking a look down the road and around the premises. The man was nowhere in sight.

"Now we're in for another delay," remarked Jack ruefully, as he gazed at the smashed window. "It seems as if we'd never get started for the moon."

"Oh, yes, we will," declared Professor Henderson. "We have some extra heavy plate glass in the shop, and we can soon put in another observation window."

"Let's get right to work then," proposed Jack. "That man may come back. Did you learn who he was, Mark?"

"No, he wouldn't tell his name, and he said he was doing this to get revenge on us for some fancied wrong. I can't imagine who he is. But let's work and talk at the same time. I'll tell you all that happened to me," which he did briefly.

Mark soon got rid of the tramp clothes, and donned an extra suit which had been packed in his trunk in the projectile. Then he helped replace the broken window, which, in spite of their haste, took nearly all the rest of the day to put in place.

"Shall we wait and start to-morrow?" asked Jack, when four o'clock came. "It will soon be dark."

"Darkness will make no difference to us," announced Professor Roumann. "Our Cardite motor will soon take us out of the shadow of the earth, and we will be in perpetual sunshine until we reach the moon. As we are all ready, we might as well start now."

They all agreed with this, and, after a final inspection of the projectile, the travellers entered it, and Jack was once more about to seal the big door.

Before he could do so there came riding into the yard, on his motorcycle, which he had claimed that afternoon, Dick Johnson.

"Wait a minute," he cried. "I've got a letter for you. It's from that man!"

"What—another thing to delay us?" cried Jack, but he called to Professor Roumann not to start the motor, and ran to take from Dick the letter which the lad held out.

"That same man who gave me the one for Mark gave me this, and he paid me a half a dollar to bring it here," said the boy.

"All right," answered Jack impatiently.

He looked at the note. It was addressed to the "Moon Travellers," and, considering that he was one, the youth tore open the envelope. In the dim light of the fading day he read the bold handwriting.

"I have fixed you," the letter began. "You will never get to the moon. I shall have my revenge. You took my brother Fred Axtell to Mars and left him there. I determined to get him back, and to that end I disguised myself as one of the boys, and got aboard. When we were safely away from the earth, I would have compelled you to go to Mars and rescue my brother. But my plan has failed. I will have my revenge, though. You will never reach the moon, even if you do get started. Beware! George, the brother of Fred Axtell, will avenge his fate!"

"The brother of the crazy machinist!" gasped Jack. "Now I understand his strange actions. He's crazy, too—he wanted to go to Mars—he says we will never reach the moon! Say, look here!" cried Jack, raising his voice. "Here's bad news! That scoundrel has put some game up on us! Maybe he's tampered with the machinery! It won't be safe to start for the moon until we've looked over everything carefully! He says he's fixed us, and perhaps he has!"

From the projectile came hurrying the would-be moon travellers, a vague fear in their hearts.

Roy Rockwood

CHAPTER XIV

OFF AT LAST

In the gathering twilight Professor Henderson read slowly the note Dick had brought. Then he passed it to Professor Roumann. The latter shook his shaggy gray hair, and murmured something in German.

"Where did you meet the man?" asked Jack of the young motorcyclist.

"About two miles down the road. He was walking along, sort of talking to himself, and I was afraid of him. He called to me, and offered me a half a dollar to deliver this message. I didn't want to at first, but he said if I didn't he'd hurt me, so I took it. Is it anything bad?"

"We don't know yet," replied Mark.

"No, that is the worst of it," added Professor Roumann. "He has made a threat, but we can't tell whether or not he will accomplish it. We are in the dark. He may have done some secret damage to our machinery, and it will take a careful inspection to show it."

"And will the inspection have to be made now?" asked Jack.

"I think so," answered Professor Henderson gravely. "It would not be safe to start for the moon and have a breakdown before we got there. We must wait until morning to begin our trip."

"It will be the safest," spoke the German, and the boys, in spite of the fact that they were anxious to get under way, were forced to the same conclusion.

"Then if we're going to camp here for the night," proposed old Andy, "what's the matter with me and the boys having a hunt for that man? We've put up with enough from him, and it's time he was punished. If we let him go on, he'll annoy us all the while, if not now, then after we get back from the moon. I'm for giving him a chase and having him arrested."

"He certainly deserves some punishment, if only for the way he treated Mark," was Jack's opinion, his chum having related how he was drugged and kept a prisoner in the secret room, and how he escaped in time to unmask the villain.

"Well," said Professor Henderson, after some thought, "it might not be a bad plan to see if you could get that scoundrel put in some safe place, where he could make no more trouble for us. I guess the lunatic asylum is where he belongs, though I can sympathize with him on account of his brother. But it was not our fault that the crazy machinist went with us to Mars. He was a stowaway, and went against our wishes, and when he got there he tried to injure us."

"Then may Mark, Andy and I see if we can find this man?" asked Jack.

"Yes, but be careful not to get separated; and don't run any risks," cautioned the professor. "Mr. Roumann and I, with the help of Washington, will go carefully over all the machinery, and every part of the projectile, to see if any hidden damage has been done. But don't stay out too late. You had better notify the police. They may be able to give you some aid, and I don't mind letting them know about it now, as we will soon be away from here, because, no matter if they do send detectives or constables spying about now, they can learn none of our secrets."

Waiting only to partake of a hasty meal, the two boys and the veteran hunter set out, Andy with his gun over his shoulder and his sharp eyes on the lookout for any sign of Axtell, though they hardly expected to find him in the vicinity of the projectile.

Taking the road, on which Dick Johnson said he had encountered the man, the two lads and Andy proceeded, making inquiries from time to time of persons they met. But no one had seen Axtell, and the insane man, for such he seemed to be, appeared to have dropped out of sight.

On into the village the searchers went, and there they reported matters to the chief of police, telling him only so much as was necessary to give him an understanding of the situation.

"I'll send a couple of my best constables right out on the case," said the chief. "We've just appointed two new ones, and I guess they'll be glad to arrest somebody."

"Let them look out that this fellow doesn't drug them and carry them away," cautioned Mark.

"Oh, I guess my constables can look out for theirselves," spoke the chief proudly.

Once more the trailers sallied forth to renew their search.

They thought perhaps they might find their man lingering in the town, but a search through the principal streets did not disclose him, and Mark proposed that they return to their home for the night, as he was tired and weary from his experience in the deserted house.

As they were turning out of the town, their attention was attracted by a disturbance on the street just ahead of them. A woman screamed, and men's voices were heard. Then came cries of: "Police! Police!"

"Some one's in trouble!" exclaimed Jack. "Let's go see what it is."

They broke into a run, and, as they approached, they saw a crowd quickly collect. It seemed to center about a man who was being held by two others, though he struggled to get away.

"Here, what's the trouble?" the boys heard a constable ask as he shouldered his way into the throng.

"This fellow tried to snatch this lady's purse and run away with it," explained one of the men who had grabbed the scoundrel. "Stand still, you brute!" he shouted at him, "or I'll shake you to pieces! Such fellows as you ought to go to the whipping-post!"

"I'll take charge of him," announced the officer. "Who is he? Does any one know?"

"Stranger in town, I guess," volunteered the other man, who had helped capture him. "Need any help, officer?"

"No, I guess I can manage him. Come along now, and behave yourself, or I'll use my club. It hasn't been tried on

Roy Rockwood

any one yet."

"That's one of the new constables, I guess," said Mark, and Jack nodded.

The crowd separated to allow the officer to take out his prisoner. As the latter walked forward in the grip of the constable, he remarked in a mild voice totally at variance with his bold act:

"Why, I only wanted a little change to pay my fare to the moon. I'm going there to look for my brother."

"Crazy as a loon," said one of the men.

"Or pretending that he is," added the officer.

"Mark!" cried Jack, pointing at the prisoner, "look!"

"The man who held me captive!" gasped Mark. "And he's wearing my clothes yet! But he's in custody now, and we needn't fear any more from him."

"Unless he gets away," said Jack.

"We'll go tell the chief who he is, and he'll keep him safe," suggested Mark, and they hurried to headquarters, reaching there just before the prisoner was brought in. The boys were assured by the chief that the man, who was evidently a dangerous lunatic, would be kept where he could do no harm. He would be arraigned later on the serious charge of attempted highway robbery, as well as of being a dangerous lunatic at large. When the boys and Andy got back, they found the two professors and Washington still going over the machinery in detail.

"Find anything wrong?" asked Jack, after they had told of the arrest of Axtell.

"No, but we will have another look in the morning," said Mr. Henderson. "Then, if we find nothing out of order, I think we will take a chance and start."

A thorough inspection by all hands the next day did not disclose anything wrong, and, a test of the motors and other machinery having shown that it was in good working shape, it was decided to leave the earth.

"At last, I think, we are really going to get under way to the moon," said Jack, as he closed the big main door. This time it was not reopened. All the stores and supplies were in place. The two professors were in the engine room. Washington White was in his galley, getting ready to serve the first meal in the air. Jack and Mark were in the pilot house, ready to do whatever was necessary and anxious to feel the thrill that would tell them the projectile had left the earth.

"All ready?" asked Professor Henderson.

"All ready," replied his German assistant.

"Then here we go!" announced the aged scientist.

He pulled toward him the main starting lever of the Cardite motor, while Professor Roumann opened the valve which admitted to the plates and cylinders the mysterious force that was to send them on their way.

"Elevate the bow!" called Professor Henderson.

"Elevated it is," answered the German, as he turned a wheel which directed the negative gravity force against the surface of the ground and tilted up the nose of the *Annihilator*, as a skyrocket is slanted in a trough before the fuse is ignited.

"Throw over the switch," directed Mr. Henderson, and the other scientist, with a quick motion, snapped it into place, amid a shower of vicious electric sparks that hissed as when hot iron is thrust into water.

"Steer straight ahead!" called Professor Henderson to Mark and Jack, who were in the pilot house. "We'll head for the moon later."

"Straight ahead it is," answered Jack.

There was a trembling to the great projectile. Up rose her sharp-pointed bow. She swayed slightly in the air. The trembling increased. The great Cardite motor hummed and throbbed. There was a crackling as from a wireless apparatus.

Then, with a rush and a roar, the big steel car, resembling an enormous cigar, soared away from the earth, like some gigantic piece of fireworks, and shot toward the sky.

"We're off!" shouted Mark.

"For the moon!" added Jack.

And the *Annihilator* soared upward and onward, while those in her never dreamed of the fearful adventures that were to befall them ere they would again be headed toward the earth.

CHAPTER XV

THE SHANGHAI MAKES TROUBLE

Remaining in the engine room long enough to see that all the motors and apparatus were working smoothly, Professor Henderson made his way to the pilot house forward, where Mark and Jack were in charge of the steering gears. The projectile could be started and stopped from there, as well as from the engine room, once the motor was set going.

"Well, boys, how does it feel to be in space once more?" asked the scientist.

"Fine," answered Mark. "But while I was shut up in that old house I feared I'd never have this chance again."

"It seems like old times again, to be flying through space," remarked Jack. "My! but we aren't making half the speed of which the projectile is capable. Why, we're only going about twenty miles a second," and he spoke as if that was a mere nothing.

"Twenty miles is some speed," observed Mark.

"The earth goes around the sun at the rate of nineteen miles a second, or about seventy-five times as fast as the swiftest cannon-ball, so you see, Jack, you are 'going some,' as the boys say."

"Yes, but we went much faster when we went to Mars. Still, no matter how fast we travel, you'd never realize it inside here."

This was true. So well balanced was the projectile, and so delicately poised was the machinery, that the terrifically fast rate of travel, rivalling that of the earth, was no more noticed than we, on this globe, notice our pace of nineteen miles a second around the sun.

"Everything seems to be all right," observed Professor Henderson, as he looked out of the plate-glass window of the pilot house into a sea of rolling mist, which represented the ether, for they had soon passed through the atmosphere of the earth, which scientists estimate to be two hundred miles in thickness.

"Are we going to move any faster than this?" asked Jack, who seemed possessed of a speed mania.

"Not right away," replied Mr. Henderson. "Professor Roumann wants to thoroughly test the Cardite motor first. Then, when he finds that it works all right, we may go faster. But we will be at the moon soon enough as it is. It is time we headed more directly on our proper way, though, so I think I will ask Mr. Roumann to step here and aid me in getting the projectile on the right course. You boys had better remain also and learn how it is done. You may need to know some time."

"I'll call the professor here, if he can leave the engine room," said Mark, and he found the German bending over some complicated apparatus. The scientist announced that the machines would run themselves automatically for a while, so he accompanied the lad back to the pilot- house.

There, consulting big charts of the heavens, and by making some intricate calculations, which the boys partly understood, the German and Mr. Henderson were able to locate the exact position of the moon, though that body was not then in sight, being behind the earth.

"That ought to bring us there inside of a week," announced Mr. Henderson, as he fastened the automatic steering apparatus in place. "The projectile will now be held on a straight course, and I hope we shall not have to change it."

"Could anything cause us to swerve to one side?" asked Jack.

"Sure," replied Mark. "Don't you remember how, in the trip to Mars, we nearly collided with the comet? If we are in danger of hitting another one of those things, or even a meteor, we'll steer out of the way, won't we?"

"Of course. I forgot about that," admitted Jack.

"Yes," declared Professor Roumann, "we'll have to be on the lookout for wandering meteors or other stray heavenly bodies. But our instruments will give us timely warning of them. Now, I think we can leave the projectile to herself while I make sure that all the machinery is running smoothly. You boys may stay here if you like, though there isn't much to see."

There wasn't. It was totally unlike taking a trip on earth, where the ever-varying scenery makes a journey pleasant. There was no landscape to greet the eye now. It was even unlike a trip in a balloon, for in that sort of air-craft, at least for a time, a glimpse of the earth can be had. Now there was nothing but a white blanket of mist to be seen, which rolled this way and that. Occasionally it was dispelled, and the full, golden sunlight bathed the projectile. The earth had long since dropped out of sight, for it required only a few seconds to put the *Annihilator* high up in a position where even the most intrepid balloonist had never ventured.

Mark and Jack sat for a few minutes in the pilot-house, looking out into the ether. But they soon tired of seeing absolutely nothing.

"I wonder what we'll do when we get to the moon?" asked Jack of his chum.

"Why, I suppose you'll make a dive for a hatful of diamonds, won't you? That is, if you still believe that Martian newspaper account."

"I sure do."

The boys found the two professors busy adjusting some of the delicate scientific instruments with which they expected to make observations on the trip, and after they reached the moon.

"What is your opinion, Professor Roumann, of the temperature at the moon's surface?" asked Mr. Henderson.

"I am in two minds about it," was the reply. "A few years ago, I see by an astronomy, Lord Rosse inferred from his observations that the temperature rose at its maximum (or about three days after full moon) far above that of boiling water."

"Boiling water!" ejaculated Mark. "Wow! That won't be very nice. I don't want to be boiled like a lobster!"

"Wait a moment," cautioned Mr. Roumann, with a smile. "Later, Lord Rosse's own investigations, and those of Langley, threw some doubts on this. There is said to be no air blanket about the moon, as there is about the earth, so that the moon loses heat as fast as it receives it; and it now seems more probable that the temperature never rises above the freezing point of water, just as is the case on our highest mountains."

"That's better," came from Jack. "We can stand a low temperature more easily than we can to be boiled; eh, Jack?"

"Sure. But I don't want to be frozen or boiled either, if I can help it. Guess I'll wear my fur suit that we brought back from the North Pole with us."

"I agree with you, Professor Roumann, about the temperature," announced Mr. Henderson, "so we must make up our minds to shiver, rather than melt. But we are prepared for that."

"What about there being no air on the moon?" asked Jack.

"Oh, we can manufacture our own oxygen," said Mark. "We can walk around with an air tank on our shoulders, as we did when we went beneath the surface of the ocean. Now, I guess—"

"Dinner am served in de dining car!" interrupted Washington White, his black face grinning cheerfully. He used to be a waiter in a Pullman, and he was proud of it. "First call fo' dinner!" he went on. "Part ob it am boiled, part am roasted, laik I done heah yo' talkin' 'bout jest now, an' part am frozed—dat's de ice cream," he added hastily, lest there be a mistake about it.

"Well, that sounds good," observed Mark. "Come on, everybody," and he led the way to the dining cabin.

They had not been at the table more than a few minutes, and had begun on the "boiled" part of the meal, which was the soup, when from the engine room there came a curious, whining noise, as when an electric motor slows up.

"What's that?" cried Professor Henderson, jumping up from his seat in alarm.

"Something wrong in the engine room," cried Mr. Roumann.

The two scientists, followed by the boys, hurried to where the various pieces of apparatus were sending the projectile forward through space. Already there was an appreciable slackening of speed.

"The Cardite motor has stopped!" cried Mr. Roumann. "Something has happened to it!"

"Can it be the result of the damage which that lunatic did?" asked Mr. Henderson.

"Perhaps," spoke Jack. "If I had him here—"

"We are falling!" shouted Mark, looking at an indicator which marked their speed and motion.

"Can't we start some other motor?" asked Jack.

At that instant from beneath the now silent Cardite machine there came a prolonged crow.

"My Shanghai rooster!" shouted Washington. "He am in dar!"

A second later the rooster scrambled out, scratching vigorously. Grains of corn were scattered about. The motor started up again, and the projectile resumed its onward way.

"The rooster stopped it!" cried Jack. "He went under it to get some corn, and he must have deranged one of the levers. Oh, you old Shanghai, you nearly gave us all heart disease!"

And the rooster crowed louder than before, while his colored owner "shooed" him out of the engine room. The trouble was over speedily, and the *Annihilator* was once more speeding toward the moon.

CHAPTER XVI

"WILL IT HIT US?"

"Well, for a trouble-maker, give me a rooster every time," spoke Jack, as, after an examination of the machinery, it was found that nothing was out of order. "How do you think it happened, Professor Henderson?"

"It never could have happened except in just that way," was the reply of Mr. Roumann. "Underneath the motor, where they are supposed to be out of all reach, are several self-adjusting levers. They control the speed, and also, by being moved in a certain direction, they will shut down the apparatus. The rooster crawled beneath the machine, an act that I never figured on, for I knew it was too small for any of us to reach with our hands or arms, even had we so desired. But the Shanghai's feathers must have brushed against the levers, and that stopped the action of the Cardite motor. However, I'm glad it was no worse."

"Yes, let's finish dinner now, if everything is all right," proposed Mark.

"How did the rooster get in here?" asked Jack.

"I 'spects dat's my fault," answered Washington. "I took him out ob his coop fo' a little exercise dis mawnin', an' he run in heah."

"That explains it, I think," said Mr. Roumann. "Well, Washington, don't let it happen again. We don't want to be dashed downward through space all on account of a rooster."

"No, indeedy; I'll lock him up good an' tight arter dis," promised the colored man.

They resumed the interrupted dinner, discussing the possibility of what might have happened, and congratulating themselves that it did not take place.

"It certainly seems like old times to be eating while travelling along like a cannon-ball," remarked Jack. "I declare, it gives me an appetite!"

"You didn't need any," retorted his chum. "But say! maybe things don't taste good to me, after what I got while that fellow Axtell had me a prisoner! Jack, I'll have a little more of that cocoanut pie, if you don't mind."

Jack passed over the pastry, and Mark took a liberal piece. Then Washington brought in the ice cream, which was frozen on board by means of an ammonia gas apparatus, the invention of Professor Henderson. The novelty of dining as comfortably as at home, yet being thousands of miles above the earth, and, at the same time, speeding along like a cannon-ball, did not impress our friends as much as it had during their trip to Mars.

"Well, we're making a little better time now," observed Mark, as he and the others rose from the table and went to the engine room. "The gauge shows that we're making twenty-five miles a second."

"We will soon go much faster," announced Professor Roumann. "I have not yet had a chance to test my Cardite motor to its fullest speed, and I think I will do so. I wish to see if it will equal my Etherium machine. I'll turn on the power gradually now, and we'll see what happens."

"How fast do you think it ought to send us along?" asked Jack.

"Oh, perhaps one hundred and twenty-five miles a second. You know we went a hundred miles a second when we headed for Mars. I would not be surprised if we made even one hundred and thirty miles a second with the Cardite."

"Whew! If we ever hit anything going like that!" exclaimed old Andy Sudds.

"We'd go right through it," finished Jack fervently. The professor was soon ready for the test. Slowly he shoved over the controlling lever. The Cardite motor hummed more loudly, like some great cat purring. Louder snapped the electrical waves. The air vibrated with the enormous speed of the valve wheels, and there was a prickling sensation as the power flowed into the positive and negative plates, by which the projectile was moved through space.

"Watch the hand of the speed indicator, boys," directed Professor Roumann, "while Professor Henderson and I manipulate the motor. Call out the figures to us, for we must keep our eyes on the valves." Slowly the speed indicator hand, which was like that of an automobile speedometer, swept over the dial.

"Fifty miles a second," read off Mark. The two professors shoved the levers over still more.

"Seventy-five," called Jack.

"Give it a little more of the positive current," directed Mr. Roumann.

"Ninety miles a second," read Mark a few moments later.

"We are creeping up, but we have not yet equalled our former speed," spoke Mr. Henderson. The motor was fairly whining now, as if in protest.

"One hundred and five miles," announced Jack.

"Ha! That's some better!" ejaculated the German. "I think we shall do it." Once more he advanced the speed lever a notch.

"One hundred and thirty!" fairly shouted Mark. "We are beating all records!"

"And we will go still farther beyond them!" cried Mr. Roumann. "Watch the gauge, boys!"

To the last notch went the speed handle. There was a sharp crackling, snapping sound, as if the metal of which the motor was composed was strained to the utmost. Yet it held together.

The hand of the dial quivered. It hung on the one hundred and thirty mark for a second, as if not wanting to leave it, and then the steel pointer swept slowly on in a circle, past point after point.

"One hundred and thirty-five—one hundred and forty," whispered Jack, as if afraid to speak aloud. The two professors did not look up from the motor. They looked at the oil and lubricating cups. Already the main shaft was smoking with the heat of friction.

"Look! look!" whispered Mark hoarsely.

"One hundred and fifty-three miles a second!" exclaimed Jack. "You've done it, Professor Roumann!"

"Yes, I have," spoke the German, with a sigh of satisfaction. "That is faster than mortal man ever travelled before, and I think no one will ever equal our speed. We have broken all records—even our own. Now I will slow down, but we must do it gradually, so as not to strain the machinery."

He slipped back the speed lever, notch by notch. The hand of the dial began receding, but it still marked one hundred and twenty miles a second.

Suddenly, above the roar and hum of the motor, there sounded the voice of Andy.

"Professor!" he shouted. "We're heading right toward a big, black stone! Is that the moon?"

"The moon? No, we are not half way there," said Mr. Henderson. "Are you sure, Andy?"

"Sure? Yes! I saw it from the window in the pilot-house. We are shooting right toward it."

"Look to the motor, and I'll see what it is," directed Mr. Henderson to his friend. Followed by the boys, he hurried to the steering tower. His worst fears were confirmed.

Speeding along with a swiftness unrivalled even by some stars, the projectile was lurching toward a great, black heavenly body. "It's a meteor! An immense meteor!" cried

Professor Henderson, "and it's coming right toward us."

"Will it hit us?" gasped Mark and Jack together.

"I don't know. We must try to avoid it. Boys, notify Professor Roumann at once. We are in grave danger!"

CHAPTER XVII

TURNING TURTLE

Together Mark and Jack leaped for the engine room. Their faces showed the fear they felt. Even before they reached it, they realized that, at the awful speed at which they were travelling, and the fearful velocity of the meteor, there might be a crash in mid-air which would destroy the projectile and end their lives.

"I wonder if we can steer clear of it?" gasped Jack.

"If it's possible the professor will do it," responded his chum.

The next instant they were in the engine room, where Mr. Roumann was bending over the Cardite motor.

"Shut off the power!" yelled Jack.

"We are going to hit a meteor!" gasped Mark.

The German looked up with a startled glance.

"Slow down?" he repeated. "It is impossible to slow down at once! We are going ninety miles a second!" He pointed to the speed gauge.

"Then there's going to be a fearful collision!" cried Jack, and he blurted out the fact of the nearness of the heavenly wanderer.

"So!" exclaimed Professor Roumann. "Dot is bat! ferry bat!" and he lapsed into the broken language that seldom marked his almost perfect English. Then, murmuring something in his own tongue, he leaped away from the motor, calling to the boys:

"Slow it down gradually! Keep pulling the speed lever toward you! I will set in motion the repelling apparatus and go to help Professor Henderson steer out of the way. It is our only chance!"

Mark and Jack took their places beside the Cardite motor, which was still keeping up a fearful speed, though not so fast as at first. To stop it suddenly would mean that the cessation of strain could not all be diffused at once, and serious damage might result.

The only way was to come gradually down to the former speed, and, while Mark kept his eyes on the indicator, Jack pulled the lever toward him, notch by notch.

"She's down to seventy-five miles a second," whispered Mark. They were as anxious now to reduce speed as they had been before to increase it.

Meanwhile Professor Roumann had set in motion a curious bit of apparatus, designed to repel stray meteors or detached bits of comets. As is well known, bodies floating in space, away from the attraction of gravitation, attract or repel each other as does a magnet or an electrically charged object.

Acting on this law of nature, Professor Roumann had, with

the aid of Mr. Henderson, constructed a machine which, when a negative current of electricity was sent into it, would force away any object that was approaching the *Annihilator*. In a few moments the boys at the Cardite motor heard the hum, the throb and crackling that told them that the repelling apparatus was at work.

But would it act in time? Or would the meteor prove too powerful for it? And, if it did, would the two scientists be able to steer the swiftly moving projectile out of the way of the big, black stone, as the old hunter called it?

These were questions that showed on the faces of the two lads as they bent over the motor.

"We're only going fifty miles a second now," whispered Jack.

Mark nodded his head. "Can't you pull the lever over faster?" he asked.

"I don't dare," replied his chum. There was nothing to do but to wait and gradually slow up the projectile as much as possible. The boys could hear the professors in the pilot-house shifting gears, valves and levers to change the course of the projectile. Andy Sudds and Washington White, with fear on their faces, looked into the engine room, waiting anxiously for the outcome.

"Hab—hab we hit it yet?" asked Washington, moving his hands nervously.

"I reckon not, or we'd know it," said the hunter.

"No, not yet," answered Jack, in a low voice. "How much are we making now, Mark?"

"Only thirty a second."

"Good! She's coming down."

Hardly had he spoken than there sounded a noise like thunder, or the rushing of some mighty wind. The projectile, which was trembling throughout her length from the force of the motor, shivered as though she had plunged into the unknown depths of some mighty sea. The roaring increased. Mark and Jack looked at each other. Washington White fell upon his knees and began praying in a loud voice. Old Andy grasped his gun, as though to say that, even though on the brink of eternity, he was ready.

Then, with a scream as of some gigantic shell from a thousand-inch rifle, something passed over the *Annihilator*; something that shook the great projectile like a leaf in the wind. And then the scream died away, and there was silence. For a moment no one spoke, and then Jack whispered hoarsely:

"We've passed it."

"Yes," added Mark, "we're safe now."

"By golly! I knowed we would!" fairly yelled Washington, leaping to his feet. "I knowed dat no old meteor could kerflumox us! Perfesser Henderson he done jumped our boat ober it laik a hunter jumps his boss ober a fence. Golly! I'se feelin' better now!"

"How did you avoid it?" asked Mark of the professor.

"With the help of the repelling machine and by changing our course. But we did it only just in time. It was an immense meteor, much larger than at first appeared, and it was blazing hot. Had it struck us, there would have been nothing left of us or the projectile either but star dust. But we managed to pass beneath it, and now we are safe."

They congratulated each other on their lucky escape, and then busied themselves about various duties aboard the aircraft. The rest of the day was spent in making minor adjustments to some of the machines, oiling others, and in planning what they would do when they reached the moon.

In this way three days and nights passed, mainly without incident. They slept well on board the *Annihilator*, which was speeding so swiftly through space—slept as comfortably as they had on earth. Each hour brought them nearer the moon, and they figured on landing on the surface of that wonderful and weird body in about three days more.

It was on the morning of the fourth day when, as Mark and Jack were taking their shift in the engine room, that Jack happened to glance from the side observation window, which was near the Cardite motor. What he saw caused him to cry out in surprise.

"I say, Mark, look here! There's the moon over there. We're not heading for it at all!"

"By Jove! You're right!" agreed his chum. "We're off our course!"

"We must tell Professor Henderson!" cried Jack. "I'll do it. You stay here and watch things."

A few seconds later a very much alarmed youth was rapidly talking to the two scientists, who were in the pilot-house.

"Some unknown force must have pulled us off our course,"

Jack was saying. "The moon is away off to one side of us."

To his surprise, instead of being alarmed, Mr. Roumann only smiled.

"It's true," insisted Jack.

"Of course, it is," agreed Mr. Henderson. "We can see it from here, Jack," and he pointed to the observation window, from which could be noticed the moon floating in the sky at the same time the sun was shining, a phenomenon which is often visible on the earth early in the morning at certain of the moon's phases.

"Will we ever get there?" asked Jack.

"Of course," replied Mr. Roumann. "You must remember, Jack, that the moon is moving at the same time we are. Had I headed the projectile for Luna, and kept it on that course, she would, by the time we reached her, been in another part of the firmament, and we would have overshot our mark. So, instead, I aimed the *Annihilator* at a spot in the heavens where I calculated the moon would be when we arrived there. And, if I am not mistaken, we will reach there at the same time, and drop gently down on Luna."

"Oh, is that it?" asked the lad, much relieved.

"That's it," replied Mr. Henderson. "And that's why we seem to be headed away from the moon. Her motion will bring her into the right position for us to land on when the time comes."

"Then I'd better go tell Mark," said the lad. "He's quite worried." He soon explained matters to his chum, and together they discussed the many things necessary to keep in mind when one navigates the heavens.

That day saw several thousand more miles reeled off on the journey to the moon, and that evening (or rather what corresponded to evening, for it was perpetual daylight) they began to make their preparations for landing. Their wonderful journey through space was nearing an end.

"I guess that crazy Axtell fellow was only joking when he said we'd never reach the moon," ventured Jack. "Nothing has happened yet."

"Only the meteor," said Mark, "and he couldn't know about that. I guess he didn't get a chance to damage any of the machinery."

"No, we seem to be making good time," went on his chum. "I think I'll go and—"

Jack did not finish his sentence. Instead he stared at one of the instruments hanging from the walls of the engine room. It was a sort of barometer to tell their distance from the earth, and it swung to and fro like a pendulum. Now the instrument was swinging out away from the wall to which it was attached. Further and further over it inclined. Jack felt a curious sensation. Mark put his hand to his head.

"I feel—feel dizzy!" he exclaimed. "What is the matter?"

"Something has happened," cried Jack.

The instrument swung over still more. Some tools fell from a work bench, and landed on the steel floor with a crash. The boys were staggering about the engine room, unable to maintain their balance.

There came cries of fear from the galley, where Washington White was rattling away amid his pots and pans. Andy Sudds was calling to some one, and from the pilot-house came the excited exclamations of Professors Henderson and Roumann.

"We're turning turtle!" suddenly yelled Jack. "The projectile is turning over in the air! Something has gone wrong! Perhaps this is the revenge of that crazy man!" and, as he spoke, he fell over backward, Mark following him, while the *Annihilator* was turned completely over and seemed to be falling down into unfathomable depths.

CHAPTER XVIII

AT THE MOON

Confusion reigned aboard the *Annihilator*. It had turned completely over, and was now moving through space apparently bottom side up. Of course, being cigar shaped, this did not make any difference as far as the exterior was concerned, but it did make a great difference to those within.

The occupants of the great shell had fallen and slid down the rounded sides of the projectile, and were now standing on what had been the ceiling. Objects that were not fast had also followed them, scattering all about, some narrowly missing hitting our friends. Of course, the machinery was now in the air, over the heads of the travellers.

This was one of the most serious phases of the accident, for the great Cardite motor was built to run while in the other position, and when it was turned upside down it immediately stopped, and the projectile, deprived of its motive power, at once began falling through space.

"What has happened? What caused it?" cried Mark, as he crawled over to where Jack sat on the ceiling, with a dazed look on his face.

"I don't know. Something went wrong. Here comes Professor Henderson and Mr. Roumann. We'll ask them."

The two scientists were observed approaching from the pilot-house. They walked along what had been the ceiling, and when they came to the engine room they had to climb over the top part of the door frame.

"What's wrong?" asked Jack.

"Our center of gravity has become displaced," answered Mr. Henderson. "The gravity machine has either broken, or some one has been tampering with it. Did either of you boys touch it?"

"No, indeed!" cried Mark, and his chum echoed his words.

"I wonder if Washington could have meddled with it?" went on the scientist.

At that moment the colored cook came along, making his way cautiously into the engine room. He was an odd sight. Bits of carrots, turnips and potatoes were in his hair, while from one ear dangled a bunch of macaroni, and his clothes were dripping wet.

"My kitchen done turned upside down on me!" wailed Washington, "an' a whole kettle ob soup emptied on my head! Oh, golly! What happened?"

The aged scientist looked toward the German. The latter was gazing up at the motionless Cardite motor over his head.

"There is but one way," he answered. "We must restore our centre of gravity to where it was before. Then the projectile will right herself."

"Can it be done?" asked Mark.

"It will be quite an undertaking, but we must attempt it. Bring some tables and chairs, so I can stand up and reach the equilibrium machine."

From where they had fallen to the ceiling, which was now the floor, Jack and Mark brought tables and chairs, and made a sort of stepladder. On this Professor Roumann mounted, and at once began the readjusting of the centre of gravity.

It was hard work, for he had to labor with his arms stretched up in the air, and any one who has even put up pictures knows what that means. The muscles are unaccustomed to the strain. The German scientist, though a strong man, had to rest at frequent intervals.

"We're falling rapidly," announced Jack, in a low voice, as he looked at the height gauge.

"I am doing all I can," answered Mr. Roumann. "I think I will soon be able to right the craft."

He labored desperately, but he was at a disadvantage, for the *Annihilator* was not now moving smoothly through space. With the stopping of the motor she was falling like some wobbly balloon, swaying hither and thither in the ether currents.

But Professor Roumann was not one to give up easily. He kept at his task, aided occasionally by Professor Henderson and by the boys whenever they could do anything.

Finally the German cried out:

"Ah, I have discovered the trouble. It is that scoundrel

Axtell! See!" And reaching into the interior of the machine he pulled out a small magnet. To it was attached a card, on which was written:

"I told you I would have my revenge!" It was signed with Axtell's name.

"This was the dastardly plot he evolved," said Professor Roumann. "He slipped this magnet into the equilibrium machine, knowing that in time it would cause a deflection of the delicate needles, and so shift the centre of gravity. He must have done this as a last resort, and to provide for his revenge in case we discovered him on board after we started. It was a cruel revenge, for had I not discovered it we would soon all be killed."

"Is the machine all right now?" asked Jack.

"It will be in a few minutes. Here, take this magnet and put it as far away from the engine room as possible."

It was the work of but a few minutes, now that the disturbing element was removed, to readjust the gravity machine, and Mr. Roumann called:

"Look out, now, everybody! We're going to turn right side up again!"

As he spoke he turned a small valve wheel. There was a clanging of heavy ballast weights, which slid down their rods to the proper places. Then, like some great fish turning over in the water, the *Annihilator* turned over in the ether, and was once more on her proper keel, if such a shaped craft can be said to have a keel.

Of course, the occupants of the space ship went slipping and sliding back, even as they had fallen ceilingward before, but they were prepared for it, and no one was hurt. From the galley came a chorus of cries, as pots and pans once more scattered about Washington, but there was no more soup to spill.

As soon as the *Annihilator* was righted, the Cardite motor began to work automatically, and once more the projectile, with the seekers of the moon, was shooting through space at their former speed. They had lost considerable distance, but it was easy to make it up.

"Well, that *was* an experience," remarked Jack, as he and his chum began picking up the tools and other objects that were scattered all about by the change in equilibrium.

"I should say yes," agreed Mark. "I'm glad it didn't happen at dinner time. That fellow Axtell is a fiend to think of such a thing."

"Indeed, he is! But we're all right now, though it did feel funny to be turned upside down."

An inspection of the projectile was made, but they could discover no particular damage done. She seemed to be moving along the same as before, and, except for the upsetting of things in the store-room, it would hardly have been known, an hour later, that a dreadful accident was narrowly averted.

Washington made more soup, and soon had a fine meal ready, over which the travellers discussed their recent experience.

"And when do you think we will arrive?" asked Jack of Mr. Henderson.

"We ought to be at the moon inside of two days now. We have not made quite the speed we calculated on, but that does not matter. I think we will go even more slowly on the remainder of the trip, as I wish to take some scientific observations."

"Yes, and so do I," added Mr. Roumann. "I think if we make fifteen miles a second from now on we will be moving fast enough."

Accordingly the Cardite motor was slowed down, and the projectile shot through space at slightly reduced speed, while the two scientists made several observations, and did some intricate calculating about ether pressure, the distance of heavenly bodies and other matters of interest only to themselves.

It was on the afternoon of the third day following the turning turtle of the *Annihilator* that Mark, who was looking through a telescope in the pilot-house, called out: "I say, Jack, look here!"

"What's the matter?" asked his chum.

"Why, we're rushing right at the moon! I can see the mountains and craters on it as plain as though we were but five miles away!"

"Then we must be nearly there," observed Jack. "Let's tell the others, Mark."

They hurried to inform the two professors, who at once left their tables of figures and entered the steering chamber. Then, after gazing through the glass, Mr. Henderson announced: "Friends, we will land on the moon in half an hour. Get ready."

Roy Rockwood

"Are we really going to be walking around the moon inside of thirty minutes?" asked Mark.

"I don't know about walking around on it," answered the German. "We first have to see if there is an atmosphere there for us to breathe, and whether the temperature is such as we can stand. But the Annihilator will soon be there."

The speed of the Cardite motor was increased, and so rapidly did the projectile approach Luna that glasses were no longer needed to distinguish the surface of the moon.

There she floated in space, a great, silent ball, but not like the earth, pleasantly green, with lakes and rivers scattered about in verdant forests. No, for the moon presented a desolate surface to the gaze of the travellers. Great, rugged mountain peaks arose all about immense caverns that seemed hundreds of miles deep. The surface was cracked and seamed, as if by a moonquake. Silence and terrible loneliness seemed to confront them.

"Maybe it's better on some other part of the surface," said Jack, in a low voice.

"Perhaps," agreed Mark. "It's certainly not inviting there."

Nearer and nearer they came to the moon. It no longer looked like a great sphere, for they were so close that their vision could only take in part of the surface, and it began to flatten out, as the earth does to a balloonist.

And the nearer they came to it the more rugged, the more terrible, the more desolate did it appear. Would they be able to find a place to land, or would they go hurtling down into some awful crater, or be dashed upon the sharp peak of some mountain of the moon?

It was a momentous question, and anxious were the faces of the two professors.

"Mr. Henderson, if you will undertake to steer to some level place, I will take charge of the motor," suggested Mr. Roumann. "I will gradually reduce the speed, and get the repelling machine in readiness, so as to render our landing gentle."

"Very well," responded the aged scientist, as he grasped the steering wheel.

The progress of the *Annihilator* was gradually checked. More and more slowly it approached the moon. The mountains seemed even higher now, and the craters deeper.

"What a terrible place," murmured Jack. "I shouldn't want to live there."

"Me either," said Mark.

"Can you see a place to land?" called Professor Roumann through the speaking-tube from the engine room to the steering tower.

"Yes, we seem to be approaching a fairly level plateau," was Mr. Henderson's reply.

"Very well, then, I'll start the repelling machine."

The Cardite motor was stopped. The projectile was now being drawn toward the moon by the gravity force of the dead ball that once had been a world like ours. Slowly and more slowly moved the great projectile.

There was a moment of suspense. Mr. Henderson threw over

the steering wheel. The *Annihilator* moved more slowly. Then came a gentle shock. The dishes in the galley rattled, and there was the clank of machinery. The Shanghai rooster crowed.

"We're on the moon at last!" cried jack, peering from an observation window at the rugged surface outside.

"Yes; and now to see what it's like," added Mark. "We'll go outside, and—"

"Wait," cautioned Professor Roumann. "First we must see if we can breathe on the moon, and whether the temperature will support life. I must make some tests before we venture out of the projectile."

CHAPTER XIX

TORCHES OF LIFE

The natural inclination of the boys to rush out on the surface of the moon to see what it was like was checked by the words of caution from Professor Roumann.

"Do you think it would be dangerous to venture outside the projectile?" asked Jack, as he looked from the window and noted the rugged, uneven surface of the moon.

"Very much so," was the answer. "According to most astronomers, there is absolutely no air on the moon, also no moisture, and the temperature is either very high or around the freezing point. We must find out what it is."

"How can we?" inquired Mark.

"I'll soon show you," went on the German. "Professor Henderson, will you kindly assist me."

When it had been decided to come to the moon in quest for the field of diamonds, certain changes had been made in the *Annihilator* to fit it for new conditions that might be met. One of these consisted of an aperture in the two sides of the projectile permitting certain delicate instruments to be thrust out, so that the conditions they indicated could be read on dials or graduated scales from within.

"We will first make a test of the temperature," said Mr. Roumann, "as that will be the easiest." Accordingly a thermometer was put outside, and those in the air-craft anxiously watched the red column of spirits. The temperature was marked as seventy-five inside the *Annihilator*, but the thermometer had not been outside more than a second before it began falling.

"Good!" exclaimed Mr. Henderson, as he noted it. "The temperature is going down. I'd rather have it too cold than too hot. We can stand a minus fifty of cold better than two hundred and twelve of heat. We have fur garments with us."

"It is still going down," remarked Jack, as he saw the red column drop down past the thirty mark.

"Below freezing," added Mark.

The spirits fell in the tube until they touched twenty-eight degrees, and there they remained.

"Twenty-eight degrees," remarked Professor Henderson. "That isn't so bad. At least, we can stand that if we are warmly clad."

"Yes, but it will be colder to-night," said Jack. For they had landed on the moon in bright sunlight.

"To-night?" questioned the German scientist, with a smile.

"Yes, it's always colder when the sun goes down," went on the lad.

"You have forgotten one thing," said Mr. Henderson, with a smile at his young protege. "You must remember, Jack, that the nights and days here are each fourteen days long—that is, fourteen of our days."

"How's that?" asked Jack.

"Why," broke in Mark, who was a trifle better student than was his chum, "don't you remember that the moon rotates on its axis once a month, or in about twenty-eight days, to be exact, and so half of that time is day and half night, just as on our earth, when it revolves on its axis in twenty-four hours, half the time is day and half the time is night."

"Sure, I ought to have remembered," declared Jack.

"Mark is right," added Mr. Henderson. "And, as we have most fortunately arrived on the moon at the beginning of the long day, we will have fourteen days of sunshine, during which we may expect the temperature to remain at about twenty-eight degrees. But now about the atmosphere." "We will test that directly," went on the German. "It will take some time longer, though."

Various instruments were brought forth and thrust out of the opening in the side of the projectile, which opening was so arranged that it was closed hermetically while the instruments were put forth. Then the readings of the dials or scales were taken, and computations made. In fact, some of what corresponded to the moon's atmosphere was secured in a hollow steel cup and brought inside the *Annihilator* for analysis.

"Well," remarked Professor Roumann, as he bent over a test tube, the contents of which he had put through several processes, "I am afraid we cannot breathe on the moon."

"Can't breathe on it?" gasped Jack. "Then we can't go out and walk around it."

"I didn't say that," resumed the German, with a smile. "I said we couldn't breathe the moon's atmosphere. In fact there is nothing there that we would call atmosphere. There is absolutely no oxygen, and there are a number of poisonous gases that would instantly cause death if inhaled."

"Then how are we to get out and hunt for those diamonds, Professor?" went on Jack. "Gee whiz! if I'd known that, I wouldn't have come. This is tough luck!"

"Maybe the professor can suggest a way out of the difficulty, boys," spoke Mr. Henderson. "It certainly would be too bad if, after our perilous trip, we couldn't get out of our cage and walk around the moon."

"I think perhaps I can discover a way so that it will be safe to venture forth," said Mr. Roumann. "But I must first conduct some further experiments. In the meanwhile suppose you boys get out some fur-lined garments, for, though it is only twenty-eight degrees, we will need to be well clad after the time spent inside this warm projectile."

"It does look as if he expected to get us out," remarked Jack, as he and his chum went to where Andy Sudds was.

"Yes, you'll get a chance to pick up diamonds after all, Jack. That is, if there are any here."

"Of course there are diamonds. You wait and see," and then, with the help of the old hunter, they took from the store-room their fur garments.

It was half an hour before the warm clothes were sorted out, and then the boys went back to where the two professors were.

"Well," asked Jack cautiously, "can we go outside?"

"I think so," answered the German cheerfully. "But you must always be careful to carry one of these with you," and he handed to each of the boys a steel rod about two feet long, at the end of which was a small iron box, with perforations in the sides and top.

"What is this?" asked Jack. "It looks like a magician's wand."

"And that is exactly what it is," said Mr. Henderson. "As there is no atmosphere fit to breathe on the moon, we have been forced to make our own, boys. You each hold what may be called torches of life. To venture out without them would mean instant death by suffocation or poison."

"And will these save our lives?" asked Mark.

"Yes," said Mr. Roumann. "In the iron boxes on those rods are certain chemicals, rich in oxygen and other elements, which, when brought in contact with the gases on the moon, will dispel a cloud of air about whoever carries them—air such as we find on our earth. So, boys, be careful never to venture out without the torches of life. I had them prepared in anticipation of some such emergency as this, and all that was necessary was to put in the chemicals. This I have done, and now, if you wish, you may go out and stroll about the moon."

CHAPTER XX

ON THE EDGE OF A CRATER

There was a little hesitation after Professor Roumann had spoken. Even though he assured them all that it would be safe to venture out on the surface of the moon, with its chilling temperature and its poisonous "atmosphere" (if such it can be termed), there was an uncanny feeling about stepping forth into the midst of the desolation that was on every side.

For it was desolate—terribly so! Not a sound broke the stillness. There was no life—no motion—as far as could be seen. Not a tree or shrub relieved the rugged monotony of the landscape. It was like a dead world.

"And to think that people may have once lived here," observed Jack, in a low voice.

"Yes, and to think that there may be people on the other side of the moon even now," added Mark. "We must take a look if it's possible."

"Well," remarked Mr. Henderson, after a while, "are we going out and see what it's like or not."

"Of course, we are," said Jack. "Come on, Mark, I'm

not afraid."

"Me either. Do we have to do anything to the torches to make them operate, Professor Roumann?"

"Merely press this lever," and the scientist showed them where there was one in the handle of the steel rod. "As soon as that is pressed, it admits a liquid to the chemicals and the oxygen gas is formed, rising all around you, like a protecting vapor. After that it is automatic."

"How long will the supply of chemical last?" inquired Jack.

"Each one is calculated to give out gas for nearly two weeks," was the reply; "possibly for a little longer. But come, I want to see how they work. Here is your life-torch, Professor Henderson, and there is one for you, too, Andy, and Washington."

"'Scuse me!" exclaimed the colored man hastily, as he started back toward the kitchen.

"Why, what's the matter?" asked Jack. "Don't you want to go out, and walk around the moon, and pick up diamonds?"

"Diamonds am all right," answered Washington, "but I jest done fo'got dat I ain't fed my Shanghai rooster to-day, an' I 'spects he's mighty hungry. You folks go on out an' pick up a few obde sparklers, an' when I gits de Shanghai fed I'll prognosticate myse'f inter conjunction wif yo' all."

"You mean you'll join us?" asked Mark.

"Dat's what I means, suah."

"Why, I do believe Washington's afraid!" cried Jack jokingly.

"Askeered! Who's afraid?" retorted the colored man boldly. "Didn't I done tole yo' dat I got t' feed my rooster? Heah him crowin' now? Yo' all go 'long, an' I'll meet yo' later," and with that Washington disappeared quickly.

"Well, he'll soon pluck up courage and come out," declared Professor Henderson. "Let him go now, and we'll go out and see what it is like on the moon."

"I hope we find those diamonds," murmured Jack, and Mark smiled.

In order not to admit the poisonous gases into the projectile, it was decided to leave the Annihilator and return to it by means of a double door, forming a sort of air lock. It was similar to the water lock used on the submarine. That is, the adventurers entered a chamber built in between the two steel walls of their craft. The interior door was then sealed shut automatically. Next the outer door was opened, and they could step directly to the surface of the moon and into the deadly atmosphere.

"Well, are we all ready?" asked Mr. Roumann, as he picked up one of the chemical torches.

"I guess so," responded Andy Sudds, who had his gun with him. "I hope I see some game. I haven't had a shot in a long while."

"You're not likely to up here," spoke Mr. Henderson. "Game is scarce on the moon, unless it's some of that green cheese Washington talked about."

They entered the air lock and fastened the door behind them. Then Professor Roumann pressed on the lever that swung open the outer portal.

"Hold your torches close to your head," he called. "The moon atmosphere may be too strong for us at first until we create a mist of oxygen about us."

Out upon the surface of the moon they stepped, probably the first earth beings so to do, though they had evidence that the inhabitants of Mars had preceded them.

For a moment they all gasped for breath, but only for a moment. Then the gas began to flow from the life-torches, and they could breathe as well as they had done while in the projectile, or while on the earth.

"Well, if this isn't great!" cried Jack, gazing about him.

"It certainly beats anything I ever saw," came from Mark.

"Wonderful, wonderful," murmured Professor Henderson. "We will be able to gain much valuable scientific knowledge here, Professor Roumann. We must at once begin our observations."

"I agree with you," spoke the German.

Andy Sudds said nothing. He was looking around for a sight of game, with his rifle in readiness. But not a sign of life met his eager eyes.

Once they were outside the projectile it was even more desolate than it had seemed when they looked from the observation windows. It was absolutely still. Not a breath of wind fanned their cheeks, for where there is no air to be heated and cooled there could be no wind which is caused by the differences of temperature of the air, the cold rushing in to fill the vacuum caused by the rising of the hot vapors. Clad in their fur-lined garments, which effectually defied the

Roy Rockwood

cold, the adventurers stepped out.

Over the rugged ground they went, gazing curiously about them. It was like being in the wildest part of the Canadian Rocky Mountains of our earth, and, in fact, the surface of the moon was not unlike the mountainous and hilly sections of the earth. There were no long ranges of rugged peaks, though, but rather scattered pinnacles and deep hollows, great craters adjoining immense, towering steeples of rocks, with comparatively level ground in between.

The life-torches worked to perfection. As our friends carried them, there arose about their bodies a cloud of invisible vapor, which, however, was as great a protection from the poisonous gases as a coat of mail would have been.

"This is great!" exclaimed Jack. "It's much better than to have to put on a diving-suit and carry a cylinder of oxygen or compressed air about on our shoulders."

They strolled away from the projectile and gazed back at it. Nothing moved—not a sound broke the stillness. There was only the blazing sunlight, which, however, did not seem to warm the atmosphere much, for it was very chilly. On every side were great rocks, rugged and broken, with here and there immense fissures in the surface of the moon, fissures that seemed miles and miles long.

"Well, here's where I look for diamonds," called Jack, as he stepped boldly out, followed by Mark. "Let's see who'll find the first sparkler."

"All right," agreed his chum, and they strolled away together, slightly in advance of the two professors and Andy, who remained together, the scientist discussing the phenomena on every side and the hunter looking in vain for something to shoot. But he had come to a dead world.

Almost before they knew it Jack and Mark had gone on quite some distance. Though they were not aware of it at that moment, it was much easier to walk on the moon than it was on the earth, for they weighed only one sixth as much, and the attraction of gravitation was so much less.

But suddenly Jack remembered that curious fact, and, stooping, he picked up a stone. He cast it from him, at the same time uttering a yell.

"What's the matter?" called Mark.

"Look how far I fired that rock!" shouted Jack. "Talk about it being easy! why, I believe I could throw a mile if I tried hard!"

"It goes six times as far as it would on the earth," spoke his chum, "and we can also jump six times as far."

"Then let's try that!" proposed Jack. "There's a nice level place over there. Come on, I'll wager that I can beat you."

"Done!" agreed Mark, and they hurried to the spot, their very walking being much faster than usual.

"I'll go first," proposed Jack, "and you see if you can come up to me." He poised himself on a little hummock of rock, balanced himself for a moment, and then hurled himself through space.

Prepared as he was, in a measure, for something strange, he never bargained for what happened. It was as if he had been fired from some catapult of the ancient Romans. Through the air he hurtled, like some great flying animal, covering fifty feet from a standing jump.

"Say, that's great!" yelled Mark. "Here I come, and I'll beat—"

He did not finish, for a cry of horror came from Jack.

"I'm going to fall into a crater—a bottomless pit! I'm on the edge of it!" yelled the lad who had jumped.

And, with horror-stricken eyes, Mark saw his chum disappear from sight beyond a pile of rugged rocks, toward which he had leaped. The last glimpse Mark had was of the life-torch, which Jack held up in the air, close to his head.

"Jack—in a crater!" gasped Mark, as he ran forward, holding his own life-torch close to his mouth and nose.

CHAPTER XXI

WASHINGTON SEES A GHOST

Advancing by leaps and bounds, and getting over the ground in a manner most surprising, Mark soon found himself on the edge of the great, yawning crater, into which his chum Jack had started to slide. I say started, for, fortunately, the lad had been saved from death but by a narrow margin.

As Mark gazed down into the depths, which seemed fathomless, and which were as black as night, he saw his friend clinging to a rocky projection on the side of the extinct volcano. Jack had managed to grasp a part of the rough surface as he slid down it after his reckless jump. He looked up and saw Mark.

"Oh, Mark, can't you save me?" he gasped. "Call Professor Henderson!"

"I'll get you up, don't worry!" called Mark, as confidently as he could. "Hold tight, Jack. What has become of your life-torch?"

"I have it here by me. I didn't drop it, and it's on a piece of the rock near my head. Otherwise I couldn't breathe. Oh, this place is fearfully deep. I guess it hasn't any bottom."

"Now, keep still, and don't think about that. Save your strength, hold fast, and I'll get you up."

But, having said that much, Mark was not so sure how next to proceed. It was going to be no easy task to haul up Jack, and that without ropes or other apparatus. Another matter that added to the danger was the necessity of keeping the life-torch close to one's face in order to prevent death by the poisonous gases.

Mark's first impulse was to hasten back and call the two professors, but he looked over the desolate landscape, and could not see them, and he feared that if he went away Jack might slip and fall into the unknown depths of the crater.

"I've got to get him out alone," decided Mark. "But how can I do it?"

He crawled cautiously nearer to the edge of the extinct volcano and looked down. A few loose stones, dislodged by his weight, rattled down the sides.

"Look out!" cried Jack quickly, "or you'll fall, too!"

"I'll be careful," answered Mark, and then he drew away out of danger, with a queer feeling about his heart, which was beating furiously. Mark had hoped to be able to make his way down the side of the crater to where his chum was and help him up. But a look at the steep sides and the uncertain footing afforded by the loose rocks of lava-like formation showed that this could not be done.

"I've got to think of a different scheme," decided Mark, and, spurred on by the necessity of acting quickly if he was to save Jack, he fairly forced his brain to work. For he saw by the strained look on his chum's face that Jack could not hold out much longer.

"I have it!" cried Mark at length. "My fur coat! I can cut it into strips of hide and make a rope. Then I can lower it down to Jack and haul him up."

He did not think, for the moment, of the cold he would feel when he stripped off the fur garment, and when it did come to him in a flash he never hesitated.

"After all, I've often been out without an overcoat on cold days," he said to himself. "I guess I can stand it for a while, and when Jack is up I can run back to the projectile and keep warm that way."

To think was to act, and Mark laid down his life-torch to take off the big fur coat. The next instant he had toppled over, almost in a faint, and, had he not fallen so that his head was near the small perforated box on the end of the steel rod, whence came the life-giving gas, the lad might have died.

He had forgotten, for the instant, the necessity of always keeping the torch close to his face to prevent the poisonous gases of the moon from overpowering him. Mark soon revived while lying on the ground, and, rising, with his torch in his hand, he looked about him.

"I've got to have my two hands to work with," he mused, "and yet I've got to hold this torch close to my face. Say, a fellow ought to have three hands if he's going to visit the moon. What can I do?"

In an instant a plan came to him. He thrust the pointed end of the steel rod in the crevice of some rocks, and it stood upright, so that the perforated box of chemicals was on a level with his face.

"There," said Mark aloud, "I guess that will work. I can use both my hands now." The plan was a good one. Next, taking off his coat, the lad proceeded to cut it into strips, working rapidly. He called to Jack occasionally, bidding him keep up his courage. "I'll soon have you out," he said cheeringly.

In a few minutes Mark had a long, stout strip of hide, and, taking his life-torch with him, he advanced once more to the edge of the crater. He stuck the torch in between some rocks, as before, and looked down at Jack.

"I—I can't hold on much longer," gasped the unfortunate lad. "Hurry, Mark!"

"All right. I'm going to haul you up now. Can you hold on with one hand long enough to slip the loop of this rope over your shoulders?"

"I guess so. But where did you get a rope?"

"I made it—cut up my fur coat."

"But you'll freeze!"

"Oh, I guess not. Here it comes, Jack. Get ready!"

Mark lowered the hide rope to his chum. The latter, who managed to get one toe on a small, projecting rock, while he held on with his right hand, used his left to adjust the loop over his shoulders and under his arms.

"Are you all ready?" asked Mark.

"Yes, but can you pull me up?"

"Sure. I'm six times as strong as when on the earth. Hold

steady now, and keep the torch close to your face."

Mark had placed some pieces of his fur coat under the rope where it passed over the edge of the mouth of the crater to prevent the jagged rocks from cutting the strips of hide.

"Here you come!" he cried to Jack, and he began to haul, taking care to keep his own head near his torch, which was stuck upright. Mark had spoken truly when he said he possessed much more than his usual strength. Any one who has tried to haul up a person with a rope from a hole, and with no pulleys to adjust the strain of the cable, knows what a task it is. But to Mark, on the moon, it was comparatively easy.

Hand over hand he pulled on the hide rope until, with a final heave, he had Jack out of his perilous position. He had pulled him up from the mouth of the crater, and the thick fur coat Jack wore had prevented the sharp rocks from injuring him. In another moment he stood beside Mark, a trifle weak and shaky from his experience, but otherwise unhurt.

"How did you happen to go down there?" asked Mark.

"Not from choice, I assure you," answered Jack. "I couldn't see the crater when I jumped, as it was hidden by some rocks, and I was into it before I knew it. But don't stand talking here. Put on my coat. I don't need it. I'm warm."

"I will not. I'm not a bit cold. But we may as well get back to the projectile, for they'll be worrying about us." Thereupon Mark broke into a run, for, now that the exertion of hauling up Jack was over, he began to feel cool, and the chilling atmosphere of the moon struck through to his bones.

In a short time the two lads were back at the *Annihilator*, where they found Professors Roumann and Henderson getting a bit anxious about them. Their adventure was quickly related, and the boys were cautioned to be more careful in the future.

"This moon is a curious, desolate place," said Mr. Henderson, "and you can't behave on it as you would on the earth. We have discovered some curious facts regarding it, and when we get back I am going to write a book on them. But I think we have seen enough for the present, so we'll stay in the rest of the day and plan for farther trips."

"Aren't we going to look for those diamonds?" asked Jack, who had almost fully recovered from his recent experience.

"Oh, yes, we will look around for them," assented Mr. Roumann. "I think, after a day or so, we will move our projectile to another part of the moon. We want to see as much of it as possible."

They sat discussing various matters, and, while doing so, Washington White peered into the living cabin.

"Has yo' got one ob dem torch-light processions t' spare?" he asked.

"Torch-light processions?" queried Mark. "What do you think this is, an election, Wash?"

"I guess he means a life-torch," suggested Jack. "Are you going out, Wash?"

"Yais, sah, I did think I'd take a stroll around. Maybe I kin find a diamond fo' my tie."

Laughing, Jack provided the colored man with one of the

torches, instructing him how to use it, and presently Washington was seen outside, walking gingerly around, as though he expected to go through the crust of the moon any moment. Pretty soon, however, he got more courage and tramped boldly along, peering about on the ground for all the world, as Mark said, as if he was looking for chestnuts.

They paid no attention to the cook for some little time until, when the boys and the two professors were in the midst of a discussion as to where would be the best place to move the projectile next, they heard him running along the corridor toward the cabin.

"Wash is in a hurry," observed Jack.

The next instant they sprang to their feet at the sight of the frightened face of the colored man peering in on them. He was as near white as a negro can ever be, which is a sort of chalk color, and his eyes were wide open with fear.

"What's the matter?" asked Jack.

"A ghost! I done seen de ghost ob a dead man!" gasped the colored man.

"A ghost?" repeated Mark.

"Yais, sah, right out yeah! He's lyin' down in a hole—a dead man. Golly! but I'se a scared coon, I is!" and Washington looked over his shoulder as though he feared the "ghost" had followed him.

CHAPTER XXII

A BREAKDOWN

At first they were inclined to regard the announcement of Washington lightly, but the too evident fright of the colored man showed that there was some basis for his fear.

"Tell us just what you saw, and where it was," said Mr. Henderson. "Was the man alive, Washington?"

"No, sah. How could a ghost be alive? Dey is all dead ones, ghosts am!"

"There are no such things as ghosts," said Mr. Henderson sternly.

"Den how could I see one?" demanded the cook triumphantly, as if there was no further argument.

"Well, tell us about it," suggested Jack.

"It were jest dis way," began Washington earnestly, and with occasional glances over his shoulder, "I were walkin' along, sort ob lookin' fer dem sparklin' diamonds, an' I didn't see none, when all on a suddint I looked down in a hole, and dere I seen HIM!" and he brought out the word with a jerk.

"Saw what—who?" asked Mr. Roumann.

"De ghost—de dead man. He were lyin' all curled up, laik he were asleep, an' when I seed him, I didn't stop t' call him t' dinner, yo' can make up yo' minds t' dat all."

"Can you show us the place?" inquired Jack.

"Yais, sah, massa Jack, dat's what I kin. I'll point it out from dish yeah winder, but I ain't g'wine dar ag'in; no, sah, 'scuse me!"

"Well, show us then," suggested Mark. "I wonder what it can be?" he went on.

"Maybe one of the people who came from Mars after the diamonds, who was forgotten and left here, and who died," said Jack.

"It's possible," murmured Mr. Henderson. "However, we'll go take a look. Get on your fur coats, boys, and take the life-torches. Will you come, Andy?"

"Sure. It's got to be more than a ghost to scare me," said the hunter.

They emerged from the projectile and walked in the direction Washington had pointed, holding their gas torches near their heads and talking of what they might see.

"This will be evidence in favor of my diamond theory," declared Jack. "It shows that the Martians were here."

"Wait and see what it is," suggested his chum.

They walked along a short distance farther, and then

Mark spoke.

"That ought to be the place over there," he said, pointing to a depression between two tall pinnacles of black rock.

Jack sprang forward, and a moment later uttered a cry of astonishment.

"Here it is!" he called. "A dead man!"

"A dead man?" echoed Professor Henderson.

"A petrified man," added Jack, in awe-struck tones. "He's turned to stone."

A few seconds later they were all grouped around the strange object—it was a man no longer, but had once been one. It was a petrified human being, a full-grown man, to judge by the size, and it was a solid image in stone, even the garments with which he had been clothed being turned to rock.

For a moment no one spoke, and they gazed in silence at what was an evidence of former life on the moon. The man was huddled up, with the knees drawn toward the stomach and the arms bent around the body, as if the man had died in agony. The features were scarcely distinguishable.

"That man was never an inhabitant of Mars," spoke Professor Henderson, in a low voice. "He is much too large, and he has none of the characteristics of the Martians."

"I agree with you," came from Mr. Roumann.

"Then who is he?" asked Jack.

"I think," said the aged scientist, "that we are now gazing on all that was once mortal of one of the inhabitants of the moon."

"An inhabitant of the moon?" gasped Mark.

"Yes; why not?" went on Mr. Henderson. "I believe the moon was once a planet like our earth—perhaps even a part of it, and I think that it was inhabited. In time it cooled so that life could no longer be supported, or, at least, this side of the moon presents that indication. The people were killed—frozen to death, and by reason of the chemical action of the gases, or perhaps from the moon being covered with water in which was a large percentage of lime, they were turned to stone. That is what happened to this poor man."

"Such a thing is possible," admitted Professor Roumann gravely.

And, indeed, it is, as the writer can testify, for in the Metropolitan Museum in New York there are the remains of an ancient South American miner, whose body has been turned into solid copper. The corpse, of which the features are partly distinguishable, was found four hundred feet down in an old copper mine, where the dripping from hidden springs, the waters of which were rich in copper sulphate, had converted the man's body into a block of metal, retaining its natural shape. The body is drawn up in agony, and there is every indication that the man was killed by a cave-in of the mine. Some of his tools were found near him.

They remained gazing at the weird sight of the petrified man for some time.

"Then the moon was once inhabited?" asked Jack at length.

"I believe so—yes," answered Professor Henderson.

"Then where are the other people?" asked Mark. "There must be more than one left. Why was this man off here alone?"

"We don't know," responded the German scientist. "Perhaps he was off alone in the mountains when death overtook him, or perhaps all his companions were buried under an upheaval of rock. We can only theorize."

"It will be something else to put in the book I am to write," said Mr. Henderson. "But, now that we have evidence of former life on the moon, we must investigate further. We will make an attempt to go to the other side of the country, and to that end I suggest that we set our projectile in motion and travel a bit. There is little more to see here."

This plan met with general approval, and, after some photographs had been taken of the petrified man, and the professors had made notes, and set down data regarding him, and had tried to guess how long he had been dead, they went back to the *Annihilator*.

"Well, did yo' all see him?" asked Washington.

"We sure did," answered Jack. "You weren't mistaken that time."

They got ready to move the projectile, but decided to remain over night where they were. "Over night" being the way they spoke of it, though, as I have said, there was perpetual daylight for fourteen days at a time on the moon.

Professors Roumann and Henderson made a few more observations for scientific purposes. They found traces of some vegetation, but it was of little value for food, even to the lower forms of animal life, they decided. There was also a little moisture; noticed at certain hours of the day. But, in the main, the place where they had landed was most desolate.

"I hope we get to a better place soon," said Jack, just before they sealed themselves up in the projectile to travel to a new spot.

As distance was comparatively small on the moon, for her diameter is only a little over two thousand miles and the circumference only about six thousand six hundred miles, the *Annihilator* could not be speeded up. If it went too fast, it would soon be off the moon and into space again.

Accordingly the Cardite motor was geared to send the big craft along at about forty miles an hour, and at times they went even slower than that, when they were passing over some part of the surface which the professors wished to photograph or observe closely.

They did not rise high into the air, but flew along at an elevation of about two hundred feet, steering in and out to avoid the towering peaks scattered here and there. Occasionally they found themselves over immense craters that seemed to have no bottom.

For two days they moved here and there, finding no further signs of life, neither petrified nor natural, though they saw many strange sights, and some valuable pictures and scientific data was obtained.

It was on the third day, when they were approaching the side of the moon which from time immemorial has been hidden from view of the inhabitants of the earth, that Jack, who was with Mark in the engine room, while the two professors were in the pilot-house, remarked to his chum: "Mark, doesn't it strike you that the water pump and the air apparatus aren't working just right?"

"They don't seem to be operating very smoothly," admitted Mark, after an examination.

"That's what I thought. Let's call Mr. Henderson. The machinery may need adjusting."

Jack started from the engine room to do this, and as he paused on the threshold there was a sudden crash. Part of the air pump seemed to fly off at a tangent, and a second later had smashed down on the Cardite motor. This stopped in an instant, and the projectile began falling. Fortunately it was but a short distance above the moon's surface, and came down with a jar, which did not injure the travellers.

But there was sufficient damage done to the machinery, for with the breaking of the air pump the water apparatus also went out of commission, and together with the breakdown of the Cardite motor had fairly stalled the *Annihilator*.

"What's the matter?" cried Professor Henderson, running in from the pilot-house, for an automatic signal there had apprised him that something was wrong.

"There's a bad break," said Jack ruefully.

"A bad break! I should say there was," remarked the scientist. "I think we'll have to lay up for repairs." And he called Mr. Roumann.

CHAPTER XXIII

LOST ON THE MOON

Notwithstanding that they were somewhat accustomed to having accidents happen, it was not with the most pleasant feelings in the world that the moon travellers contemplated this one. It meant a delay, and a delay was the one thing they did not want just now.

They desired to get to the other side of the moon while the long period of sunshine gave them an opportunity for observation. True there was some time yet ere the long night of fourteen days would settle down, but they felt that they would need every hour of sunshine.

"Well, it's tough luck, but it can't be helped," said Mark.

"No, let's get right to work," suggested Jack.

They got out their tools and started to repair the two pumps. It was found that the Cardite motor was not badly damaged, one of the negative electrical plates merely having been smashed by a piece of the broken connecting rod of the air pump. It was only a short time before the motor was ready to run again.

But it could not be successfully operated without the air and water pumps, and it was necessary to fix them next. New gaskets were needed, while an extra valve and some sliding gears had to be replaced.

"It's an all day's job," remarked Professor Henderson.

But many hands made light work, and even Washington and Andy were called upon to do their share. By dinner time the work was more than half done, and Professor Roumann, announced that he and Mr. Henderson would finish it if Jack and Mark would take a look at the exterior of the projectile, to see if any repairs were needed to that.

The boys found that some of the exterior piping had become loosed at the joints, because of the jar of the sudden descent, and, taking the necessary tools outside, while they stuck their life-torches upright near them, they labored away.

At four o'clock the two lads had their task completed, and at the same time Professor Henderson announced that the air and water pumps were now in good shape again.

"Then let's get under way at once," suggested Mr. Roumann. "We have lost enough time as it is. Hurry inside, boys, and we'll start."

The two chums were glad enough to do so, and in a few minutes they were again moving through the air toward the unknown portion of the moon.

Below the travellers, as they could see by looking down through a plate-glass window in the floor of the projectile, were the same rugged peaks, the same large and small craters that had marked the surface of the moon from the time they had first had a glimpse of it. There was an uninteresting monotony about it, unrelieved by any save the very sparest vegetation.

"I am beginning to think more and more that we will find people on the other side of this globe," remarked Mr. Roumann, as he made an observation through a telescope.

"What strengthens your belief?" inquired Mr. Henderson.

"The fact that the vegetation is growing thicker. There are many more plants below us now than there were before. This part of the moon is better able to support life than the portion we have just come from."

This seemed to be so, but they were still some distance from the opposite side of the moon.

"I don't see anything of those diamonds you talked so much about, Jack," said Mark, with a smile, a little later. "I guess all the Reonaris you get you can put in a hollow tooth."

"You wait," was all Jack replied.

The projectile was slowed up to permit the two professors to make some notes regarding a particularly large and deep crater, and a few minutes later when Mark, who was in the engine room, attempted to speed up the Cordite motor it would not respond.

"Humph! I wonder what's wrong?" he asked of Jack.

"Better call Mr. Roumann, and not try to fix it yourself," suggested his chum, when, in response to various movements of the lever, the machine seemed to go slower and slower.

The German came in answer to the summons.

"Ha!" he exclaimed, "that motor is broken again. We shall have to stop once more for repairs. I shall need to take it all apart, I fear. Get me the negative plate remover, will you, Mark?"

The lad went to the tool chest for it. He opened the lid and fumbled about inside.

"It doesn't seem to be here," he announced.

"What! the negative plate remover not there?" cried the professor. "Why, it must be. It is one of the new tools we got, and it has not been used for anything; has it?".

"Oh, by Jinks!" cried Jack suddenly.

"What's the matter?" asked his chum.

"That plate remover! Don't you remember you and I had it when we were fixing the pipes outside the projectile, when we had the other breakdown? We must have left it back there on the ground."

Jack and his chum gazed blankly at each other.

"I guess we did," admitted Mark dubiously.

"And it is the only one we have," said Mr. Roumann. "We need it very much, too, for the projectile can't very well be moved without it."

"How can we get it?" asked Jack. "I'm sorry. It was my fault."

"It was as much mine as yours," asserted Mark. "I guess it's up to us to go back after it. It isn't far. We can easily walk it."

There seemed to be nothing else to do, and, after some discussion, it was decided to have the two boys walk back after the missing tool, which was a very valuable one.

"Take fresh life-torches with you," advised Mr. Henderson, "and you had better carry some food with you. It may be farther back than you think, and you may get hungry."

"I guess it will be a good thing to take some lunch along," admitted Jack. "And some water, too. We can't get a drink here unless we come to a spring, and we haven't seen any since we arrived."

"I'll go with you, if you don't mind," said Andy. "I may see something to shoot."

The three of them, each one carrying a freshly charged vapor-torch, a basket of food and a bottle of water, started off, well wrapped in their fur coats. Andy had a compass to enable them to make their way back to where the tool was left, for, amid the towering peaks and the valley-like depressions, very little of the level surface of the moon could be seen at a time.

They walked on for several hours, every now and then hoping that they had reached the place where the projectile had been halted, and where they expected to find the tool. But so many places looked alike that they were deceived a number of times.

At length, however, they reached the spot and found the instrument where Jack had carelessly dropped it. They picked it up and turned to go back, when Andy Sudds saw a large crater off to one side.

"Boys, I'm going to have a look down that," he said. "It may contain a bear or wildcat, and I can get a shot."

"Guess there isn't much danger of a bear being on the moon," said Mark, but the old hunter leaned as far over the edge of the crater as he dared.

"No, there's nothing here," he announced, with almost a sigh, and he straightened up. As he did so there came a tinkling sound, as if some one had dropped a piece of money.

"What's that?" asked Jack.

"By heck! It's the compass!" cried Andy. "It slipped from my pocket when I stooped over. Now it's gone!"

There was no question of that. They could hear the instrument tinkling far down in the unfathomable depths, striking from side to side of the crater as it went down and down.

"We'll never see that again," spoke Mark dubiously. "Can we get back to the projectile without it?" asked Jack.

"Oh, I fancy I can pick my trail back," answered the hunter. "It isn't going to be easy, for there are no landmarks to guide me, but I'll do my best. I ought to have known better than to put a compass in that pocket."

It was not with very light hearts that they started back, and for a time they went cautiously. Then, as they seemed to get on familiar ground, they increased their pace and covered several miles.

"Say," remarked. Jack, as he sat down on a big stone. "I don't know how the rest of you feel, but I'm tired. We've come quite a distance since we picked up that tool."

"Yes, farther than it took us to find it after we left the projectile," added Mark. "I wonder if we're going right?"

The two boys looked at Andy. He scratched his head in perplexity.

"I can't be sure, but it seems to me that we came past here," he said. "I seem to remember that big rock."

"There are lots like it," observed Jack.

"Suppose we try over to the left," spoke Mark, after they had rested for ten minutes.

They swerved in that direction, and, after keeping on that trail for some time, and becoming more and more convinced that it was the wrong one, they turned to the right. That did not bring them to familiar ground, and there was no sight of the projectile.

"Let's go straight ahead," suggested Andy, after a puzzled pause. "I think that will be best."

"Well, which way is straight ahead?" asked Mark.

"That's so, it is hard to tell," admitted the hunter. "I wish I hadn't lost that compass."

They wandered about for an hour longer. They could seem to make no progress, though they covered much ground. Suddenly Jack called out:

"Say, we've been going around in a circle!"

"In a circle?" asked Mark.

"Yes," went on his chum. "Here's the very rock I sat down on a while ago. I remember it, for I scratched my initials on it."

Jack pointed out the letters. There was no disputing it. They had made a complete circle. For a moment they maintained silence in the face of this alarming fact. Then Mark exclaimed:

"I guess we're lost!"

"Lost on the moon!" added Jack, in an awestruck voice, and he gazed on the chill and desolate scene all about them; the great pinnacles of rocks, in fantastic form; the immense black caverns of craters on either hand; the sickly green vegetation.

"Lost on the moon!" whispered Mark, and there was not even an echo of his voice to keep them company. Only a chill, desolate silence!

CHAPTER XXIV

DESOLATE WANDERINGS

For a moment the three stood helplessly there and stared at each other. They could scarcely comprehend their situation at first. Then, with a glance at the cold and quiet scene all about them, a look up at the sun, which was the only cheerful object in the whole landscape, Jack observed: "Oh, I say, come on now, don't let's give up this way! We have only taken a wrong turn, and I'll wager that the projectile will be just around the corner. Come on," and he started off.

"Yes," said Mark, "that's the trouble. There are so many corners, and we have taken so many wrong turns, that we're all confused. I think the best thing to do will be to stay here a while and pull ourselves together."

"That's right," spoke old Andy. "Many a time in the woods I've got all confused-like, and then I'd sit down and think, and I'd get on the right path in a few minutes after."

"The trouble here is," said Jack, "that there are no woods. If there were we might know how to get out of them. But think of it! Lost on the moon, in the midst of a whole lot of queer mountain peaks, and big holes that would hold half a dozen cities of the United States at the same time, and never know it! This is a fearful place to be lost in!"

"I'm not going to admit that we're lost," declared Mark stoutly.

"Hu! You're like the Indian," spoke Jack. "The Indian who got lost in the woods. He insisted that it wasn't he who was lost, that it was his wigwam that couldn't be found. He knew where he himself was all the while. That's our case, I suppose. We're here, but the projectile is lost."

"Ha! ha!" laughed Andy Sudds. "That's a pretty good joke!"

"But not being able to find the projectile is no joke," went on Mark, who always took matters more seriously than did his chum. "What are we going to do?" he added. "We can't stay here like this."

"Maybe we'll have to," declared Jack. "We certainly can't get off the moon—at least, not until we reach the projectile, and I'd like to discover those diamonds before we go back."

"Hu! Those diamonds!" exploded Mark. "I think this whole thing is a wild-goose chase, anyhow! If it hadn't been for those diamonds we wouldn't have come to the moon. I don't believe there are any diamonds here, anyhow."

"Well, I can't prove it to you now, but I will before we get back," asserted Jack. "We'll be wearing diamonds, as the song says."

"Diamonds aren't going to keep us warm when we're free-zing," went on Mark, who seemed bound to look on the dark side, "and we can't eat 'em when we're hungry. A lot of good they'll do us if we do find them!"

"Oh, cheer up!" suggested Jack cheerfully. "And, speaking of eating, what's the matter with having some lunch? What did we bring it along for if we're not going to eat? Let's begin."

His good spirits were contagious, not that Andy needed any special cheering up, but Mark did. In a few minutes they were seated on some rugged rocks, and, with their life-torches stuck in cracks, so that the perforated metal boxes of chemicals would be on a level with their faces, they opened the baskets they had been fore-sighted enough to bring with them.

"Why, I feel better already," asserted Jack, as he munched some sandwiches which Washington White had made. "As soon as we've finished we'll have another hunt for the projectile, and I'll wager that we'll find it."

"I wouldn't finish if I were you," suggested Andy, who was eating sparingly.

"Finish what?" asked Jack.

"All your lunch. You see," the old hunter went on, "we may find the projectile, and, again, we may not. I'm inclined to think we're not so very far from it, but we may be some time locating it in among all these peaks and craters. So it will be the best plan to save some of our lunch and drinking water until—well, until we're hungry again," and he carefully put back into his basket the remains of the food.

"You don't mean to say you think we'll be all day finding the Annihilator, do you?"

Jack paused, with a sandwich half way to his mouth as he asked this question.

"Well, it's best to be on the safe side," spoke Andy guardedly. "We may find it, and, again, we may not. Save your powder against the time of need, I say—by powder meaning victuals and drink. We can't drop in a restaurant up here, and I don't see much game to shoot, and I should hate to eat such fodder as this," and he poked with his foot some sickly green vines, growing on the ground.

The boys' faces, which had become more cheerful, assumed a serious look. Jack stopped eating at once and placed back in the basket his remaining sandwiches. He also corked up the bottle of water, which was kept from freezing by means of a fur pouch in which it was carried.

"If there's a possibility of being lost some time," spoke Mark, "we'd better figure out just how long our food will last," and he examined the contents of his basket.

Fortunately Washington White, with a knowledge of the appetites of the chums, had filled the baskets with lavish hands. There was, they found, food enough to last them three days, if they ate sparingly, and there was enough water for half that time, providing they only took small sips when thirsty. But they had noticed, in one or two places, little pools of liquid, which they had not tasted, but which might prove to be drinking water. Certainly they would need more if they were destined to remain away from the projectile for very long.

"Well, then," observed Mark, when the food calculation was over, "it appears that we can remain lost for about three days, at the most."

"Oh, but we'll be back home—I mean in the projectile—long before that," declared Jack.

"I wish I was sure of that," murmured Andy with a dubious shake of his head.

"Well, let's move on again," suggested Jack. "We feel better now, and maybe we'll have better luck."

They started off, tramping over the rugged surface of the moon, while the sun shone with tepid heat down on them. They had to go this way and that to avoid the immense fissures in the ground or the yawning craters, which loomed deep, and in awful silence, in their path. Sometimes they climbed small mountains or crawled in and out of small craters, slipping and stumbling.

They were not cold, for their fur garments kept them comfortably warm, and there was no wind to make the freezing temperature search through the crevices of their clothing. But it was the desolate silence, the utter absence of any form of life save the pale green vegetation that got on their nerves. It was like being in a dead world—on a planet that seemed about to dissolve into space.

They began their further search for the projectile with hope in their hearts, but this gradually gave way to despair as they wandered on over the desolate surface, and saw nothing but the same rugged peaks, the same yawning caverns and the innumerable craters, large and small.

On they wandered, looking on all sides for the missing projectile, but they had no glimpse of it. Even climbing to one of the high peaks, whence they had a view of the surrounding country, afforded them no trace of the *Annihilator*, They were utterly lost.

Old Andy, who, by reason of his experience as a trapper and hunter, had taken the lead, came to a halt. He looked around helplessly. He did not know what to do.

"Well, boys," he remarked at length, "I don't like to say it, but I can't seem to get anywhere. I give up."

"Give up?" murmured Jack, in blank dismay.

"Yes, for the time being," said the old man. "I'm all played out. I guess we all are. We must have a rest. Here's a sort of cave. Let's crawl in and have a sleep. Then maybe we can do something to-morrow—no, not to-morrow, for they don't have that on the moon, where the day is fourteen days long—but after we sleep we may be able to find our way back. Anyhow, I've got to get some sleep," and without another word the old hunter went into the cave, and, fixing his life-torch near his head, where the fumes from it would dissipate the poisonous gases of the moon, he closed his eyes, and was soon in slumber.

"I—I guess we'd better do the same," said Jack, and Mark nodded. They were both sick at heart.

CHAPTER XXV

THE PETRIFIED CITY

For a time, after they had entered the cave, which was in the side of a rugged mountain, the boys talked in low tones of their perilous situation. For that it was perilous they both knew. Had they been on the earth, lost in some desolate part of it, away from civilization, their plight, would have been bad enough with what little food they possessed.

But on the far-off moon—the dead moon, which contained no living creatures save themselves, as far as they could tell—with no form of animal life that might serve to keep them from starving, with only the scantiest of vegetation, their situation was most deplorable.

"And then there's another thing," said Mark, as if he was cataloguing a list of their troubles.

"What is it?" asked Jack. "I guess we have all the troubles that belong to us, and more, too."

"Well, what are we going to do when the life-torches give out, and we can't breathe any more?" asked Mark dubiously.

"Well, I guess it'll be all up with us then, if we don't starve to death in the meanwhile," answered Jack. "But I'm afraid we will get out of food before the torches are exhausted. They were freshly filled before we started out after that tool, and they'll last for two weeks. So we don't have to worry about that.

"By Jinks! this is all my fault, anyhow, it seems. If I hadn't seen that item in the Martian paper about the diamonds, we never would have come here, and if I hadn't left that tool on the ground outside of the projectile we wouldn't have had to come back after it, and we wouldn't have become lost. So I guess it's up to me, as the boys say."

"Oh, nonsense!" exclaimed Mark, who, as soon as he heard his chum blaming his own actions, was ready to shoulder part of the responsibility himself. "We all wanted to come to the moon," he went on, "and, as for leaving the tool and forgetting it, I'm as much at fault as you are. Let's go to sleep, and maybe we'll feel better when we wake up."

It was a new role for Mark—to be cheerful in the face of difficulties—and Jack appreciated it. They stretched out on the hard, rocky floor of the cavern, taking care to fix their life-torches so that the fumes would dispel the poisonous gases. Then the two lads joined Andy in slumberland.

Meanwhile, as may be imagined, those aboard the projectile were very anxious about the fate of the two boys and the hunter. They could not understand what delayed them, and, though they guessed the real cause, after several hours had passed, there was nothing the two scientists could do.

They could not move the projectile until it had been repaired, and this could not be done, without the tool—at least, they did not believe so then. Nor did Mr. Henderson and the German think it would be safe to start out in search of the wanderers.

"For," said Mr. Henderson, "if we went we would easily get lost amid these peaks ourselves, and they are so much alike and in such numbers that there is no distinguishing feature about them. We had better stay here in charge of the *Annihilator* until the boys and Andy come back. They can't be away much longer now."

So worn out and exhausted were the boys and the hunter that they slept for several hours in the cave, and the rest did them good. They awoke in better spirits, and, after a frugal meal and a sip of the fast- dwindling water, they started off once more to locate the projectile.

"I'm a regular amateur hunter to go and lose my compass," complained old Andy. "I ought to have it fastened to me, like a baby does the rattle-box. I ought to kick myself," and he accepted all the blame for their misadventure. But the boys would not suffer him to thus accuse himself, and they insisted that they would shortly be with the two professors and Washington in the *Annihilator* once more.

"Well, it can't come any too soon," said Jack, "for I am beginning to feel the need of a square meal and a big drink of water."

"So am I," said Mark, "but let's not think of it."

All that day they wandered on, crossing the rugged mountains, climbing towering peaks, and descending into deep valleys. At times they skirted the lips of craters, to look shudderingly into the depths of which made them dizzy, for the bottoms were lost to sight in the black gloom that enshrouded the yawning holes.

Their food was getting less and less, and what there was of it was most unpalatable, for the bread was stale and dry, though the meat kept perfectly in that freezing temperature. How they longed for a hot cup of coffee, such as Washington used to make! and how they would have even exchanged their chance of filling their pockets with the moon diamonds for a good meal, such as was so often served in the projectile!

On and on they went. Once, as they were crossing the lip of a great crater, Mark became dizzy, and would have fallen had not Jack caught him. Mark had forgotten, for the moment, and had lowered his life- torch, so that his mouth and nose were not enclosed in the film of vapor that emanated from the perforated box.

"You must be careful," Andy warned them.

"What's the use?" asked Mark despondently. "I don't believe we'll ever find the projectile."

"Of course we will!" exclaimed Jack. "I know we can't be far from it, only we can't see it because of the mountains. If we only had some way of letting them know where we are, they could signal to us."

"By gum!" suddenly exclaimed Andy.

"What's the matter?" asked Jack, for the old hunter was capering about like a boy.

"Matter? Why, the matter is that I'm a double-barrelled dunce," was the answer. "Look here; do you see that?" and he held up his rifle.

"Sure," replied Jack, wondering if their sufferings and worry had made the old hunter simple-minded.

"What is it?" asked Andy, shaking it in the air.

"Your rifle," answered Mark, looking at Jack in surprise.

"Of course," answered the hunter, "and a rifle is made to be fired off, and here I've been carrying mine for nearly three days now, and I haven't shot it once. You wanted a signal to make the folks in the projectile hear us. Well, here it is I I guess they can hear this, and when they do they can come and get us, for we don't seem able to reach them. I'll just fire some signal shots."

"That's the stuff!" cried Jack, and Andy proceeded to discharge his rifle.

The report the gun made in that quiet place was tremendous, and the effect was curious, for, there being no air in the ordinary acceptance of the word, there was no echo. It was as if one had hit two shingles together. Merely a loud, sharp sound, and then an utter silence, the vibrations being swallowed up instantly.

"Do you think they can hear that?" asked Andy.

"It sounds loud enough," answered Jack. "Shoot some more," which the old hunter did. They wandered on still farther, firing at intervals all that day, but there came no answering report or calls to direct them to the projectile. They climbed once more to the tops of towering peaks, but there they found their range of vision limited by peaks still higher, while there were great valleys, in one of which, whether near or far they could not tell, they knew, the *Annihilator* was hidden.

They had almost lost track of time now, and they did not know how far they had wandered. They had sought out lonely caves to sleep in when they were so weary they could go no farther, and they had sat about on bleak rocks shivering, and had eaten their scanty meals—shivering because in spite of their fur garments they were cold, as they did not eat enough to keep their blood properly circulating. They could not when they did not have the food to eat!

Andy used up all but a few of his cartridges in firing signals, but to no purpose. Their water was all but gone, and of their food only enough remained for a day longer, though their life-torches still gave forth plenty of vapor.

"Well, what's to be done?" asked Jack, as they sat about, looking helplessly at one another.

"Might as well give up," suggested Mark bitterly.

"Give up? Not a bit of it!" cried Andy, as cheerfully as he could. "Let's keep on. We'll find the projectile sooner or later."

So they kept on. It was while making their way between two great mountain peaks that towered above their heads on either side, thousands of feet up, making a sort of natural gateway, that Jack, who was in the lead, cried out in astonishment at the sight that met his gaze when he had passed the pinnacles.

"Look!" he shouted, pointing forward.

What he indicated was a great crater—larger and deeper than any they had yet met with. It seemed a mile across, and, if gloom and darkness were any indications, it was a hundred miles deep.

But it was not the size of the great hole in the ground, not its fearful gloom, that attracted their attention. What did was a great natural or artificial bridge of stone that was thrown across the middle of it from edge to edge. A bridge of stone that spanned the abyss; a roadway, fifty feet wide, which reached into some unknown land, connecting it with the desolate country in which our friends had been wandering.

"A bridge of stone across the cavern," said Jack, "but see. Here is a house of stone. This was the guard-house, I'll wager—the guardhouse at the entrance to some city, and that bridge is the means by which the inhabitants entered and left. Maybe we are at the edge of the inhabited part of the moon!"

His words thrilled them. They pressed forward to the beginning of the bridge across the crater. They looked into the stone hut. Clearly it had been made by hands, for it was composed of blocks of stone, neatly fitted together. Jack's theory seemed confirmed.

Mark peered into the house, and uttered a cry of alarm.

"There's a petrified man in there!" he gasped.

Jack and Andy looked in at the open window. They saw, sitting at a table, which was also of rock, a man, evidently a soldier, or rather he had been, for he was nothing but stone now, like the hut in which he dwelt.

The wanderers looked at each other with fear on their faces. What dreadful mystery were they about to penetrate? "Let's cross the bridge," suggested Jack, in a low voice. "Maybe this marks the end of desolation. Perhaps we may find life and food across the crater."

"But—but the petrified man!" gasped Mark.

"What of it? He won't hurt us. Maybe there are live men, who will take care of us, beyond there," and Jack pointed across the bridge of stone.

There was nothing to keep them where they were—in the land of desolation. They could not live much longer there, with no food and water. To pass on over the crater seemed the only thing to do.

"Come ahead," called Jack boldly. They followed him. They kept in the middle of the road, for to approach the edge, where there was a sheer descent of so many feet that it made them dizzy to think of it, filled them with terror. On they hurried until, in a short time, they had crossed the great chasm.

The road over the crater came to an end between two peaks, similar to those at the beginning. Jack was the first to pass them, and as he emerged he once more uttered a cry—a cry of fear and wonder.

And well he might, for in a valley below the wanderers there was a city. A great city, with wonderful buildings, with wide streets well laid out—a city in which figures of many men and women could be seen—little children too! A fair city, teeming with life, it seemed!

But then, as they looked again, struck by the curious quiet that prevailed, they knew that they were gazing down on a city of the dead—a city where the inhabitants had been turned to stone, even as had the soldier on guard in his lonely hut.

They had come upon a petrified city of the moon!

CHAPTER XXVI

SEEKING FOOD

"Well, if this isn't the limit!" burst out Jack, when he had stood and contemplated the silent city for several moments, which also his companions did. "After all our wanderings and troubles, when we do find a place, it isn't any good to us. I don't suppose there is a square meal in the whole town! Isn't it wonderful, though—every person turned to stone!"

"Wonderful!" gasped old Andy. "I never saw anything like it in all my life! What do you reckon did it, boys?"

"The same thing that turned the man in the hut, and the one Washington thought was a ghost, into stone," answered Mark. "There was a rain of some lime-water, or a liquid charged with similar chemicals, and the people were turned to rocks."

It was uncanny, and for a moment they hesitated on the edge of the city, which lay in a sort of cup-like valley, surrounded on all sides by towering peaks of the moon mountains. The bridge over which they had come afforded the only entrance to the city, and in times of war (provided the inhabitants of the moon ever fought) the passage must have been well guarded.

It was evidently a time of peace when the calamity that turned the inhabitants to stone came upon them, for only one soldier was in the guard hut—doubtless being there merely to give an alarm, or possibly to keep out undesirable strangers.

"Well, are we going to stand here all day?" asked Jack of his companions, when they had contemplated the silent city for five minutes longer.

"I say, let's go down there and see what we can find. I'm getting hungry."

"There'll be nothing there to eat," declared Mark. "If there ever was anything, it's now stone. Think of a loaf of bread like a brick, and a chunk of meat like some great rock!"

"Let's go down, anyhow," added Andy, and they advanced.

As they got down into the streets, the weird effect came over them more strongly. It was as if they had suddenly entered some large town, and at their advent every living person had been turned into an image.

"Wonderful, wonderful!" murmured Jack.

"I've read of the uncovering of the ancient buried cities, and how they found women in the kitchen baking bread, and men at their work, but this goes ahead of that, for here the people are not dust—they are statues!"

"It certainly is wonderful," agreed Mark. "I only wish the two professors could see this. They could write several books about it. This proves that the moon was once inhabited, though it is dead now. The projectile should have come to this part of the moon."

"Maybe they'll bring it here, when we get back and tell them what we've seen," suggested Jack.

"Yes, if we ever do get back," went on his chum, with a return of his gloomy thoughts.

The strangeness of the scenes all about them can scarcely be imagined. Think of looking at a city street teeming with life, men and women hurrying here and there, dogs running about, children at their play, and then suddenly seeing that same street become as dead as some mountain, with the people represented as stones on that same mountain, and you can get some idea of what our friends looked upon.

Here was a woman, looking in a store window, probably at some bargains, though even the very window and store itself was now stone, and the woman was like a block of marble. Near her was a little child, also turned to stone, and there were a number of men, standing together on a street corner as if they had been talking politics when the calamity overtook them.

There were shops where the workers had been turned to stone at their benches, there were houses at the windows of which stone faces peered out, and there were parks on the benches of which sat men, women and children, stiff and solid—creatures of stone! Truly it was a city of the dead!

The wanderers walked about, seeing new wonders on every side. They spoke in whispers at times, as though at the sound of a loud voice the silent ones would awaken and resume the occupations or pleasures they had left off centuries ago.

Another strange part of it was that the people were not so very different from those of the earth. They were exactly the same in size and feature, but their clothing, as nearly as could be told from the stone garments, seemed of a bygone fashion, such as was in vogue hundreds of years ago. There were no horses observed, though there were stone dogs and cats, and the shops given over to the sale of food contained in the windows what seemed to be chunks of meat, loaves of bread, and pies and cakes, though now they were only pieces of rock.

"It's just as if one of our cities and the people in it should be suddenly petrified," said Mark. "It's almost like the earth up here; only they don't seem to have gotten to trolley cars yet."

"Maybe they would if the moon hadn't cooled off when it did, and killed them all," suggested Jack. "But, I say, let's get down to something more practical than theorizing."

"What, for instance?" asked Mark.

"Looking for something to eat," went on Jack. "I'm nearly starved, and I have only half a sandwich left. I want to eat it, yet, if I do, I don't know where I'm going to get more. And as for water, I'd give a handful of diamonds, if I had them, for half a glass of even warm water."

"Yes, we do need food and water badly," said Andy.

"Then let's look for it," suggested Jack. "If we can find food in any of these houses or shops, I don't believe the people will care if we take it."

"Find food here?" cried Mark. "Why, you must be crazy! All the food is turned to stone, and what isn't would be spoiled! Why, no one has been alive here for thousands and thousands of years!"

"That's nothing," asserted Jack. "Don't you remember

reading how, in the arctic regions, they have found the bodies of prehistoric elephants and mastodons encased in blocks of ice, where they have been for centuries. The meat is perfectly preserved because of the cold. And what of the grains of wheat they find in the coffins of Egyptian mummies? Some of that is three thousand years old, yet it grows when they plant it, and they can make bread of it.

"Now, maybe we can find some wheat or something to eat in some of these houses. If there's meat, it will be perfectly preserved, for the temperature is below freezing."

"That may be," admitted Mark, convinced, in spite of himself, "but it's turned to stone, I tell you."

"The outside part may be," said Jack, "but if we can crack off the outside layer of stone we may find some good meat inside. I'm going to look, anyhow."

"That's not a bad idea!" cried Andy with enthusiasm. "Think of having a loaf of bread and some beefsteak thousands of years old. I suppose they had beefsteak here," he added cautiously.

"Some kind of meat, anyhow," agreed Jack. "Well, let's look for a place that was once a restaurant or hotel, and we'll see what luck we have. Come on."

They walked along the silent streets, with their silent occupants, and finally Jack found what he was seeking. It was an eating place, to judge by the appearance, and at tables inside were seated stone men and women.

"Back to the kitchen!" cried Jack with enthusiasm. "There's where we'll find food, if there is any!"

"It'll be all stone," declared Mark, but he and Andy followed Jack.

They came to the place where was what appeared to be a stove. It was more like a brick oven, however, than a modern range, though in dishes that were now stone something was being cooked when the catastrophe occurred.

"There's meat, I'll wager!" cried Jack, pointing to several objects on a table. They looked like chunks of beef, but when Mark struck them with the end of his life-torch they gave forth a sound as if a rock had been tapped.

"What did I tell you?" Mark asked, "Nothing but rocks. And the bread is also a stone," he added bitterly.

"You're right," admitted Jack, with a sigh. "And I'm getting hungrier than ever." They all were. For days they had been without sufficient food, and now, when it was almost within their reach, they were denied it by this curious trick of nature. With pale and wan faces they gazed at each other, wetting their parched lips, for they had some time since taken the last of their scant supply of water, and they were very thirsty.

"I guess it's all up with us," murmured Mark. "We'll soon be like these poor people here—blocks of stone."

"If we only could change this meat back into it's original shape," spoke Jack musingly, smiting his fist against a block of beef.

Suddenly Andy uttered a cry.

"I have it!" he fairly shouted.

"What?" asked Jack.

"I have a plan to get meat out of this hunk of stone!"

The two boys gazed at the old hunter as though they thought he had lost his reason, but, chuckling gleefully, Andy took from his pouch several cartridges, and proceeded to remove the wads, and pour the powder from the paper shells out on the stone table.

"I'll have some meat for us," he muttered. "We shan't starve now!"

CHAPTER XXVII

THE BLACK POOL

"What are you going to do, Andy?" asked Jack, as he watched the old hunter.

"What am I going to do? Why, I'm going to blast out some of this meat, that's what I'm going to do! I heard you boys talking about elephants and other things being preserved for centuries in a cake of ice, and, if that's true, why won't the meat in this petrified city be preserved just as well? It's always below freezing here, and that's cold enough."

"But the meat has turned to stone," objected Mark.

"Only the outside part of it, to my thinking," answered Andy. "I believe that inside these lumps of rock we'll find good, fresh meat!"

"But how are you going to get it?" asked Jack.

"Just as I told you—blast it out with some of the powder from my cartridges. I used to be a miner before I turned hunter, and when we wanted gold we used to fire a charge in some rocks. Now we want meat, and I'm going to do the same thing. I'll put some powder underneath this block of stone that looks as if it was a chunk of roast beef, and we'll see what happens. It's lucky I saved some of my cartridges."

While he was talking the old hunter had taken some of the powder and put it back in one of the paper shells. Then, making a fuse by twisting some powder grains in a piece of paper he happened to have in his pocket, he inserted it in the improvised bomb, using some dirt and small stones with which to tamp down the charge. He discovered a crack in the big stone, which they hoped would prove to be a chunk of roast beef, and Andy put the cartridge in that.

"Look out now, boys," he called, "I'm going to light the fuse. I didn't make a heavy charge, but it might do some damage, so we'll go outside."

They hurried from the place, with its silent guests and waiters, and reached the street. A moment later there sounded a dull explosion.

"Now, let's see what we've got!" called Jack.

Back to the kitchen they ran, the two boys in the lead.

"Why—why—the stone has disappeared!" cried Jack, in disappointment, as he glanced all around.

"Yes, but look here," added Mark. "Here are bits of meat," and he picked up from the stone table some scraps of meat.

"Is it really roast beef?" cried Jack. "Good to eat?"

Mark smelled of it. Then he put the morsel cautiously to his lips. The next instant it had disappeared. It was proof enough.

"Good! I should say it was good!" exclaimed Mark. "I wish there was more of it! What happened to the rock of meat, Andy?"

"I used too heavy a charge, and it blew all to pieces. I'll know better next time. There are lots more chunks of meat, and we'll soon have a feast. I'll make another bombshell."

He worked rapidly while Jack sampled some of the shreds of meat that had been scattered about by the explosion. The beef was perfectly cooked, and in spite of its great age it was as fresh and palatable as frozen meat ever is. Besides the heat generated by the explosion had partly thawed it, so that there was no trouble in chewing it.

Once more came the explosion, a slight one this time, and when the adventurers re-entered the kitchen they found that what had been a lump of stone had been broken open, and the middle part, like the kernel of a nut, was sweet and good. It was cooked, so they did not have to eat it raw.

"Say, maybe this isn't good!" exclaimed Jack, chewing away. "It's the best ever!"

"And there's enough in this city to keep us alive for months, if we can't find the projectile in that time," declared Andy.

"Don't you think we will?" asked Mark.

"Of course, but I was only just mentioning it. Now, eat all you want, boys, I have quite a few cartridges left. I didn't fire away as many as I thought I did, and we can blast out a dinner any time we want it. So eat hearty!"

They needed no second invitation, and for the first time in several days they had enough to eat. It was comfortable in the petrified restaurant, too, for they could move about without carrying their life- torches constantly in their hand. The gases from the perforated boxes filled the rooms, and were not quickly dispelled by the poisonous vapors as they were outside, so they could walk around in comparative freedom.

"Now, if we could only blast out a loaf of bread, we'd be all right," said Jack. They found some petrified loaves, but on breaking one open it was found to be stone all the way through.

Spurred on by an overwhelming thirst, they wandered about the dead city, but found no moisture. They tried to chew some of the pale green vegetation that grew more plentiful on this side of the moon, but it was exceedingly bitter, and they could not stand it, though there was some juice in it.

They crossed the city, and wandered out into the country beyond. It appeared to have been a fertile land before the stone death settled down on it. They saw farmers in the fields, turned into images, beside the oxen with which they had been plowing. But nowhere was there a sign of water. Had it not been for a frozen rice pudding, they would have perished that first day in the stone city.

As it was, they dragged out a miserable existence, eating from time to time of the blasted meat. But even this palled on them after a while, for their lips were parched and cracked, and their tongues were swollen in their mouths.

"I can't stand this any longer!" cried Jack.

"What are you going to do?" asked Mark.

"Go out and look for water. There must be some in the

country outside if there isn't any in this city. I'm going to have a look. Besides, if I'm going to die, I might as well die while I'm busy. I'm not going to sit here in this dreadful place and give up."

His words urged them to follow him, and, with lagging steps, for they were weak and faint, they went from the restaurant, which they had made their home since coming to the petrified city.

Out into the open fields they went, but their search seemed likely to be in vain. Between times of looking for the water they scanned the sky for a sight of the projectile, which, hoping against hope, they thought they might see hovering over them. But there was no sight of it.

They came to a vast, level plain, girt with mountains, a lonesome place, where there was no sign of life. Listlessly they walked over it.

Suddenly Andy, who was in the lead, uttered a cry and sprang forward. The boys ran to him, and found the old hunter gazing into the depths of a great black pool, which filled a depression in the surface of the moon. It was a small crater, and was filled, nearly to the top, with some black liquid, which gloomily reflected back the light of the sun.

"I'm going to have a drink!" cried Andy, and before the boys could stop him he threw himself face downward at the edge of the black pool.

CHAPTER XXVIII

THE SIGNAL FAILS

"Stop! Don't drink that! It may be poison!" yelled Jack.

"Pull him back!" shouted Mark, and together they advanced on the old hunter. They tried to drag him away from the black pool, but Andy shook them off.

"Let—me—alone!" he gasped, as he bent over the uninviting liquid and drank deeply. "It's water, I tell you—good water —and I'm almost— dead—from—thirst!"

"Water? Is that water?" cried Jack.

"Well, it's the nearest thing to it that I've tasted since I've been lost on the moon," spoke Andy, as he slowly arose. "My, but that was good!" he added fervently.

"But—water?" gasped Mark. "How can there be water here?"

"Taste and see," invited the old hunter.

They hesitated a moment, and then followed his example. The liquid—water it evidently had once been—had a peculiar taste, but it was not bad. By some curious chemical

Roy Rockwood

action, which they never understood, the liquid had been prevented from evaporating, nor was it frozen or petrified as was everything else on the moon.

What gave the liquid its peculiar black color they could not learn. Sufficient for them that it was capable of quenching their thirst, and they all drank deeply and refilled their bottles.

"Now, I feel like eating again," spoke Andy, "We can take some of this back with us, and have a good meal on blasted meat. Whenever we get thirsty we'll have to make a trip back here for water."

The boys agreed with him. They examined the black pool. It appeared to be filled by hidden springs, though there was no bubbling, and the surface was as unruffled as a mirror. The liquid was not very inviting, being as black as ink, but the color appeared to be a sort of reflection, for when the water, if such it was, had been put into bottles it at once became clear, nor did it stain their faces or hands.

"Well, it's another queer thing in this queer moon," said Jack. "I wish the two professors could see this place. They'd have lots to write about."

"I wonder if we'll ever see them again?" asked Mark.

"Sure," replied Jack hopefully. "We'll fill our lunch baskets, take a lot of water along, and have another hunt for the projectile soon."

They did, but with no success. For several days more they lived in the petrified city, the meat encased in its block of stone, which Andy blasted from time to time, and the black water keeping them alive. From time to time they went out in the surrounding country, looking for the projectile. But they could not find the place where they had left it, nor could they find even the place where they had picked up the lost tool that had cost them so much suffering. They were more completely lost than ever. They crossed back and forth on the bridge over the crater chasm, and penetrated for many miles in a radius from that, marking their way by chipping off pieces of the rocky pinnacles, as they did not want to leave the petrified city behind.

From some peaks they caught glimpses of other towns that had fallen under the strange spell of the petrification. Some were larger and some smaller than the one they called "home."

Jack proposed visiting some of them, thinking they might find better food, but Mark and Andy decided it was best to stay where they were, as they were nearer the supposed location of the projectile.

"I think they'll manage to fix it up somehow, so it will move," said Andy, "and then they'll come to look for us. I hope it will be soon, though."

"Why?" asked Jack, struck by something in the tone of the old hunter.

"Because," replied Andy, "I am afraid our life-torches won't last much longer. Mine seems to be weakening. I have to hold it very close to my face now to breathe in comfort, while at first the oxygen from it was so strong that I could hold it two feet off and never notice the poisonous moon vapors."

This was a new danger, and, thinking of it, the faces of the boys became graver than ever. Death seemed bound to get them somehow.

Two more days went by. They had now been lost on the moon over a week. Each one now noticed that his life-torch was weakening. How much longer would they last? They dared not answer that question. They could only hope.

The sun, too, was moving away from them. Soon the long night would set in. By Mark's computation there was only three more days of daylight left. What would happen in the desolate darkness?

As they were returning from the black pool, with their water bottles filled, and put inside the fur bags to prevent the frost from reaching them, Mark happened to gaze over across a line of towering peaks. What he saw caused him to gasp in astonishment.

"Jack! Andy! See!" he whispered hoarsely, pointing a trembling finger at the sky.

There, outlined against the cloudless heavens, was a long, black shape, floating through the air about two miles distant.

"The projectile! The *Annihilator!*" yelled Jack. "Shout! Call to them! Wave your hands! Andy, fire your gun! They have started off, and they can't see us. We must make them hear!"

Together they raised their voices in a mighty shout. The old hunter fired his gun several times. They waved their hands frantically.

But the projectile never swerved from its course. On it moved slowly, those in it paying no heed to the wanderers, for they did not hear them. Andy fired his gun again, but the signal failed, and a few minutes later the *Annihilator* was lost to sight behind a great peak.

CHAPTER XXIX

THE FIELD OF DIAMONDS

Dumbly the wanderers gazed at each other. They could not comprehend it at first. That the projectile, on which their very lives depended in this dead world of the moon, should float away and leave them seemed incredible. Yet they had witnessed it.

"Do—do you really think we saw it—saw the *Annihilator*, Mark?" asked Jack in a low voice, after several minutes had passed.

"Saw it? Of course, we saw it. We've seen the last of it, I'm afraid. But what do you mean?"

"I—I thought maybe I was out of my head, and I only saw a vision," answered Jack. "You know—a sort of mirage. It was real, then?"

"Altogether too real," spoke Andy Sudds grimly. "They didn't see us nor hear us. We're left behind!"

"But can't we do something?" demanded Mark. "Let's start off and try to catch them. They were going slow."

"The wonder to me is how they moved at all," said Jack. "I thought the machinery wouldn't work until we got back with the lost tool."

"Probably the two professors found some way of patching up the motor," was Mark's opinion, and later they found that this was so.

For some time they remained staring in the direction in which the projectile had vanished, as if they might see it reappear, but the great steel shell did not poke its sharp nose in among the towering peaks which hid it from view. Probably it was many miles away now.

"Well," remarked old Andy at length, "we've got to make the best of it. We won't have many more days of light, and we must gather what food we can, put it where we can find it in the dark, and also bring in some water from the black pool. We can store that in some of the stone tables. By turning them upside down they will make good troughs, and it won't freeze. We must work while we have light, for soon the long night will come."

The sight of the projectile going away seemed to take the heart out of all of them, and they did not know what to do. For some time they remained there idly, until Andy roused the boys to a sense of their responsibility by urging upon them the necessity of getting together a store of meat and water.

As they had about exhausted the limited food supply in the ancient restaurant, they sought and found another and larger one. There they had the good fortune to come upon some whole sides of beef and lamb, which were petrified on the outside, but which, when they had blasted off the outer shell of stone, gave them good food.

They made several trips to the black pool, and brought in all the liquid they could, for they did not want to have to go outside the petrified city into the wild and desolate country beyond, after the dismal night had settled down. They feared they would become lost again.

Their lonely situation seemed to grow upon them. The appalling silence all about terrified them. The weird sight of the petrified men and women in the petrified city got on their nerves.

They had done all they could. A store of meat had been blasted out and put away. It would keep outside of the stone shell now, for the weather was getting colder with the advent of the long night.

This fact worried them. With the temperature at twenty-eight when the sun was shining, what might it not fall to in the darkness? The terrible cold of the arctic regions might be nothing compared to the frostiness of the dead moon in the shadow. Their fur garments, thick as they were, might be no more protection than so much paper. And they had no means of making a fire, nor anything to burn on one had they been capable of kindling it, for Andy had used the last of his cartridges to blast with, and where everything was petrified there was no wood.

Then, too, their life-torches were giving out. The emanations of oxygen were weaker, and they had to hold them almost under their noses to breathe the vital vapor.

One day, or rather what corresponded to a day, for they had lost all track of time, Andy Sudds arose from the stone bench on which their meager meal had been served. He started from the restaurant where they had taken up their abode.

"Where are you going?" asked Jack.

"I'm going to make one last attempt to find the projectile before it gets too dark," answered the hunter. "We can go out, look around for several hours, and get back before darkness sets in. We might as well do it as sit here doing nothing. Then, too, we can bring in some more water. We'll need all we can store away."

"I'll go with you," volunteered Jack, and Mark, not wanting to be left alone in the dead city, followed. Carrying their life-torches and wrapping their fur garments closely about them, for it had grown much colder, they sallied forth.

They found a thin film of ice on the black pool, showing that it would probably freeze when it got cold enough, though the ordinary temperature of thirty-two degrees had not affected it. They filled their water bottles, and then Andy proposed that they take a new path—one they had not tried before.

They hardly knew where they were going, but ever as they tramped on they cast anxious looks upward to see if they might descry the projectile hovering over them. But they did not see it.

Jack had taken the lead, and was walking along, glancing idly about. He came to a place where two peaks were so close together that it was all he could do to squeeze through. But the moment he had passed the defile and looked out on a broad, level field, he came to a sudden stop. His companions, who pressed after him, saw him rub his eyes and shake his head, as if disbelieving the evidence of what lay before him. Then Jack murmured: "It can't be true! It can't be true!"

"What?" called Mark.

"There! Those," answered his chum. "See, the field is covered with diamonds! We have found the diamonds of the moon—the field of Reonaris that the men of Mars discovered! There are the diamonds—millions of them!"

"Diamonds!" exclaimed Mark. He squeezed through the defile, and stood beside Jack. Before him in the fading light of the sun was a broad field, girt around with towering cliffs, and the surface of the field was covered with white stones.

Jack sprang forward and gathered up a double handful. He let them run through his fingers in a sparkling stream. Old Andy came up to the boys.

"They're only glass or crystals," he said.

"They are *not* glass or crystals!" declared Mark, who had made a study of gems. "I should say they were diamonds, probably meteoric diamonds, very rare and valuable. Why, there is the ransom of a thousand kings spread out before us!"

He fell upon his knees and began to scoop up the gems. His chum was making a little heap of the stones.

"The ransom of a thousand kings!" murmured Jack. "More diamonds than in all the world—and I'd give my share for a good ham sandwich!"

CHAPTER XXX

BACK TO EARTH—CONCLUSION

At any other time the discovery of such a vast store of wealth would have set the wanderers half wild with joy. Now they only accepted the fact dully, for the perils of their situation overburdened them. As Jack had said, they needed food more than the gems, for at best the supply they had blasted out could not last long, and when that was gone where were they to get more, for there were no more cartridges, and the rending force of powder was needed to open the rocky meat.

"I knew we'd find the diamonds," murmured Jack, as he began to fill the pockets of his fur coat. "I'm right, after all, Mark, you see."

"Yes, but what good will it do us? What's the good of even carrying any away. We can never use them."

"That's so," agreed Jack, in a low voice. "I might as well leave them here."

But somehow the desire to pick up gems which, when they were cut and polished, would rival many of the famous diamonds of history was too strong to be resisted. Though he was afraid he would never get back to earth to enjoy them,

Jack could not help putting in his pockets a goodly supply of the largest of the precious stones. Andy did the same, and Mark, in spite of his gloomy feelings, stuffed his pockets. They worked with their torches held close to their faces, and in the search for the better stones they literally walked over millions of dollars' worth of the gems.

For there, stretched out before them, was an actual field of diamonds. As Mark had said, they were of meteoric origin, that is, a meteor had burst over that particular portion of the moon, and the chemical action had created the diamonds, which had fallen in a shower in the field.

"If you boys have all you want, then let's get back to the city," suggested Andy. "No telling when it will be night now."

They followed his advice, and soon were going back by way of the black pool. It seemed more lonesome than ever, after the excitement of discovering the field of diamonds, and even Jack, glad as he was to have his theory vindicated, got tired of referring to it. His triumph meant little to him now.

They were at the entrance to the petrified city. As they were about to go in, ready to hide themselves in the deepest part of the restaurant, away from the terrible cold and appalling darkness they felt would soon be upon them, Mark came to a sudden halt. He glanced quickly up into the air and cried out: "Hark!"

"What's the matter?" asked Jack, as they stood in a listening attitude.

"I heard a noise," whispered Mark. "It sounded—I'm sure it sounded—like the crackling of the wireless motor waves of the projectile. Listen!"

Faintly through the silence came a sound as if there was a discharge of an electric current. It increased in volume, and there was a faint roaring in the atmosphere.

"It's her—it's the *Annihilator!*" shouted Jack, leaping about.

"Wait," counselled Andy, who dreaded the terrible disappointment should the boys be mistaken. The sound came nearer. The crackling could plainly be made out now. The sun was out of sight, but there was still the glow which follows sunset.

The boys were eagerly scanning the heavens, Their hearts beat high with hope. Suddenly, in the olive-tinted sky just above a range of rugged peaks, a black shape loomed. A black shape, as of a great cigar, pointed at both ends. It shot into full view.

"The projectile!" yelled Jack.

"The *Annihilator!*" gasped Mark.

"Thank Heaven, they have found us in time!" exclaimed Andy fervently, and the three stretched out their arms toward the craft from which they had been parted so long. It was as if they tried to pull it down to them.

"Do they see us?"

"Will they pass us by?"

"Make a noise so they'll hear us!"

"Wave to them!"

"Oh, if they leave us now!"

Questions, ejaculations and entreaties came rapidly from the lips of the wanderers. They raised their voices in a shout. They leaped up and down. They wildly waved their hands and life-torches.

Then, to their inexpressible joy, they saw the course of the projectile change. It was headed toward them, and a few minutes later it settled slowly to the ground about half a mile away.

"Come on!" cried Jack! "We must hurry to them, or soon it will be too dark to see them, or for them to find us. It's our last chance; don't let's lose it!"

He sprang forward, the others after him, and together they ran toward the projectile. They could see the two professors and Washington White emerging from the steel car, waving their hands.

On rushed the lost wanderers, over the rough stones, skirting the great cliffs, falling into small craters, crawling out again, just missing several times being precipitated into yawning caverns, and stumbling over petrified bodies that strewed the ground.

Ever did they hasten onward though, increasing their speed. They came to a great crater that lay between them and the projectile, but fortunately there was across the middle of it a natural bridge of stone. But it was narrow—scarcely wide enough for one at a time.

"We can never cross on that!" cried Mark, halting.

"We've got to!" shouted Jack, and he sprang fearlessly forward, fairly running over the narrow path, which had a sheer descent of thousands of feet on either side.

Mark, though fearful that he would become dizzy and fall, followed Andy. They were soon across the narrow bridge, and speeding on toward the *Annihilator*. Five minutes later they had reached it, and were being wildly welcomed by the two professors and Washington White, who had advanced to meet them.

"I 'clar t' goodness-gladness!" exclaimed the colored man, "I am suttinly constrained t' espress my approbation ob de deleterous manner in which yo' all has come back t' dis continuous territory."

"Do you mean you're glad to see us, Wash?" asked Jack.

"Dat's what I done said," was the answer, with a cheerful grin, "an' I might also remark dat dinner am serbed in de dinin' car."

"Hurrah!" cried Jack. "That's the best news I've heard in a week. No more blasted beef for mine! Give me ham and eggs!"

"But what happened to you? Where have you been? We have searched all over for you, and were just giving you up for dead, and going back to the earth," said Professor Henderson. "We caught sight of you at the last minute."

"Oh, you mustn't go back until you go to the field of diamonds!" cried Jack, and then by turns he and Mark and Andy told of their terrible adventures while they were lost on the moon.

On their part Professors Roumann and Henderson stated how they had waited in vain for the return of the wanderers, and had then, by strenuous work, managed to make the necessary repairs without the missing tool. Then they set out to discover the lost ones, but succeeded only just in time, for it was now quite dusk.

"An' did yo' all really discober dem sparklers?" asked Washington, as he served what the boys thought was the finest dinner they had ever tasted.

"We sure did," replied Jack. "Here are a couple for that red necktie of yours," and he passed over two big diamonds.

It did not take long to move the projectile to the field of the sparkling gems, and by means of a powerful search-light enough were soon gathered up to satisfy even Washington White, who declared that he would be the best decorated colored man in Bayside when they got back. The two professors made what observations they could in the petrified city in the fast-gathering darkness, and then, having taken a petrified man into the projectile with them to deposit in a scientific museum in which Professor Roumann was interested, the *Annihilator* was sealed shut.

And it was only just in time, for with the suddenness of an eclipse intense darkness settled down, and the temperature, as indicated by a thermometer thrust outside, showed a drop of a hundred degrees.

"We never could have lived out there," said Jack.

"Well, we'll soon be back on earth," observed Mark, and a little later the Cardite motor was out in operation, and the journey back to this world begun.

Little of moment happened on the return trip. The boys went more into detail about their wanderings, and told how they had managed to live during the time they were lost. The two professors and Washington spoke of their worry and anxiety, and their vain search for the wanderers.

As they were anxious to get back home, the motor was speeded to the limit, and in much less time than they had made the trip to the moon they had arrived in sight of the earth again. As they did not want to create too much excitement, they hovered about in the air over Bayside until dark, when they gently descended almost in the very spot from which they had started.

"Well," remarked Jack, as he stepped out on the earth once more, "it was quite an experience to go to the moon, and I suppose being lost there wasn't the worst thing that could happen to us, but all the same I'm glad to be back."

"So am I," declared Mark. "It was worth while going," and he felt of his pocketful of diamonds.

"We certainly made some very valuable scientific obser-vations," asserted Mr. Henderson, "and we will be able to prove that the moon was once inhabited."

Washington White was carefully lifting out his Shanghai rooster, which was uttering loud crows. As soon as he had set the fowl on the ground, the colored man started off.

"Where are you going?" asked Mark.

"I'm going t' a jewelery shop t' hab my diamonds made inter a stick-pin fo' my red necktie," was the answer.

"Oh, you'd better wait until morning," suggested Professor Henderson.

They gathered about the table in the cozy dining room of their home, while Washington got a meal ready. Every one was talking about what a wonderful trip they had had.

"The only trouble is," said Jack, "that we've been to about all the interesting places in this universe now. I wonder where we can go next?"

"I'm going to bed right after supper," announced Mark. "Maybe I'll discover a new land in my dreams."

The moon voyagers had a great store of gems, and, as they did not wish to bring down values by disposing of them, they only sold a few, which, because of their great size and brilliancy, brought a large price. Several jewelers wanted to know where the diamonds came from, but the secret was well kept. Most of the gems were used for scientific purposes, but Mark and Jack gave some to certain of their friends.

The petrified man proved a great curiosity, and a history of it, in two large volumes, can be seen in the museum where the body is exhibited. Professor Henderson wrote the account, and also published quite an extensive history of the trip to the moon, which was considered by scientists and laymen to be a most remarkable journey.

But, though our friends had been to many strange places, it was reserved for them to have yet still more wonderful adventures, though for a time after returning from the moon they remained at home, the two professors busy over their scientific work, and the boys engaged with their studies, while Andy occasionally went hunting, and Washington got the meals and, between times, fed his rooster and admired the diamonds in his red necktie. And now we will bid our friends good-by.

Choose from Thousands of 1stWorldLibrary Classics By

A. M. Barnard
Ada Leverson
Adolphus William Ward
Aesop
Agatha Christie
Alexander Aaronsohn
Alexander Kielland
Alexandre Dumas
Alfred Gatty
Alfred Ollivant
Alice Duer Miller
Alice Turner Curtis
Alice Dunbar
Allen Chapman
Alleyne Ireland
Ambrose Bierce
Amelia E. Barr
Amory H. Bradford
Andrew Lang
Andrew McFarland Davis
Andy Adams
Angela Brazil
Anna Alice Chapin
Anna Sewell
Annie Besant
Annie Hamilton Donnell
Annie Payson Call
Annie Roe Carr
Annonaymous
Anton Chekhov
Archibald Lee Fletcher
Arnold Bennett
Arthur C. Benson
Arthur Conan Doyle
Arthur M. Winfield
Arthur Ransome
Arthur Schnitzler
Arthur Train
Atticus
B.H. Baden-Powell
B. M. Bower
B. C. Chatterjee
Baroness Emmuska Orczy
Baroness Orczy
Basil King
Bayard Taylor
Ben Macomber
Bertha Muzzy Bower
Bjornstjerne Bjornson

Booth Tarkington
Boyd Cable
Bram Stoker
C. Collodi
C. E. Orr
C. M. Ingleby
Carolyn Wells
Catherine Parr Traill
Charles A. Eastman
Charles Amory Beach
Charles Dickens
Charles Dudley Warner
Charles Farrar Browne
Charles Ives
Charles Kingsley
Charles Klein
Charles Hanson Towne
Charles Lathrop Pack
Charles Romyn Dake
Charles Whibley
Charles Willing Beale
Charlotte M. Braeme
Charlotte M. Yonge
Charlotte Perkins Stetson
Clair W. Hayes
Clarence Day Jr.
Clarence E. Mulford
Clemence Housman
Confucius
Coningsby Dawson
Cornelis DeWitt Wilcox
Cyril Burleigh
D. H. Lawrence
Daniel Defoe
David Garnett
Dinah Craik
Don Carlos Janes
Donald Keyhoe
Dorothy Kilner
Dougan Clark
Douglas Fairbanks
E. Nesbit
E. P. Roe
E. Phillips Oppenheim
E. S. Brooks
Earl Barnes
Edgar Rice Burroughs
Edith Van Dyne
Edith Wharton

Edward Everett Hale
Edward J. O'Biren
Edward S. Ellis
Edwin L. Arnold
Eleanor Atkins
Eleanor Hallowell Abbott
Eliot Gregory
Elizabeth Gaskell
Elizabeth McCracken
Elizabeth Von Arnim
Ellem Key
Emerson Hough
Emilie F. Carlen
Emily Bronte
Emily Dickinson
Enid Bagnold
Enilor Macartney Lane
Erasmus W. Jones
Ernie Howard Pie
Ethel May Dell
Ethel Turner
Ethel Watts Mumford
Eugene Sue
Eugenie Foa
Eugene Wood
Eustace Hale Ball
Evelyn Everett-green
Everard Cotes
F. H. Cheley
F. J. Cross
F. Marion Crawford
Fannie E. Newberry
Federick Austin Ogg
Ferdinand Ossendowski
Fergus Hume
Florence A. Kilpatrick
Fremont B. Deering
Francis Bacon
Francis Darwin
Frances Hodgson Burnett
Frances Parkinson Keyes
Frank Gee Patchin
Frank Harris
Frank Jewett Mather
Frank L. Packard
Frank V. Webster
Frederic Stewart Isham
Frederick Trevor Hill
Frederick Winslow Taylor

Friedrich Kerst
Friedrich Nietzsche
Fyodor Dostoyevsky
G.A. Henty
G.K. Chesterton
Gabrielle E. Jackson
Garrett P. Serviss
Gaston Leroux
George A. Warren
George Ade
Geroge Bernard Shaw
George Cary Eggleston
George Durston
George Ebers
George Eliot
George Gissing
George MacDonald
George Meredith
George Orwell
George Sylvester Viereck
George Tucker
George W. Cable
George Wharton James
Gertrude Atherton
Gordon Casserly
Grace E. King
Grace Gallatin
Grace Greenwood
Grant Allen
Guillermo A. Sherwell
Gulielma Zollinger
Gustav Flaubert
H. A. Cody
H. B. Irving
H. C. Bailey
H. G. Wells
H. H. Munro
H. Irving Hancock
H. R. Naylor
H. Rider Haggard
H. W. C. Davis
Haldeman Julius
Hall Caine
Hamilton Wright Mabie
Hans Christian Andersen
Harold Avery
Harold McGrath
Harriet Beecher Stowe
Harry Castlemon
Harry Coghill
Harry Houidini

Hayden Carruth
Helent Hunt Jackson
Helen Nicolay
Hendrik Conscience
Hendy David Thoreau
Henri Barbusse
Henrik Ibsen
Henry Adams
Henry Ford
Henry Frost
Henry James
Henry Jones Ford
Henry Seton Merriman
Henry W Longfellow
Herbert A. Giles
Herbert Carter
Herbert N. Casson
Herman Hesse
Hildegard G. Frey
Homer
Honore De Balzac
Horace B. Day
Horace Walpole
Horatio Alger Jr.
Howard Pyle
Howard R. Garis
Hugh Lofting
Hugh Walpole
Humphry Ward
Ian Maclaren
Inez Haynes Gillmore
Irving Bacheller
Isabel Cecilia Williams
Isabel Hornibrook
Israel Abrahams
Ivan Turgenev
J. G.Austin
J. Henri Fabre
J. M. Barrie
J. M. Walsh
J. Macdonald Oxley
J. R. Miller
J. S. Fletcher
J. S. Knowles
J. Storer Clouston
J. W. Duffield
Jack London
Jacob Abbott
James Allen
James Andrews
James Baldwin

James Branch Cabell
James DeMille
James Joyce
James Lane Allen
James Lane Allen
James Oliver Curwood
James Oppenheim
James Otis
James R. Driscoll
Jane Abbott
Jane Austen
Jane L. Stewart
Janet Aldridge
Jens Peter Jacobsen
Jerome K. Jerome
Jessie Graham Flower
John Buchan
John Burroughs
John Cournos
John F. Kennedy
John Gay
John Glasworthy
John Habberton
John Joy Bell
John Kendrick Bangs
John Milton
John Philip Sousa
John Taintor Foote
Jonas Lauritz Idemil Lie
Jonathan Swift
Joseph A. Altsheler
Joseph Carey
Joseph Conrad
Joseph E. Badger Jr
Joseph Hergesheimer
Joseph Jacobs
Jules Vernes
Julian Hawthrone
Julie A Lippmann
Justin Huntly McCarthy
Kakuzo Okakura
Karle Wilson Baker
Kate Chopin
Kenneth Grahame
Kenneth McGaffey
Kate Langley Bosher
Kate Langley Bosher
Katherine Cecil Thurston
Katherine Stokes
L. A. Abbot
L. T. Meade

L. Frank Baum
Latta Griswold
Laura Dent Crane
Laura Lee Hope
Laurence Housman
Lawrence Beasley
Leo Tolstoy
Leonid Andreyev
Lewis Carroll
Lewis Sperry Chafer
Lilian Bell
Lloyd Osbourne
Louis Hughes
Louis Joseph Vance
Louis Tracy
Louisa May Alcott
Lucy Fitch Perkins
Lucy Maud Montgomery
Luther Benson
Lydia Miller Middleton
Lyndon Orr
M. Corvus
M. H. Adams
Margaret E. Sangster
Margret Howth
Margaret Vandercook
Margaret W. Hungerford
Margret Penrose
Maria Edgeworth
Maria Thompson Daviess
Mariano Azuela
Marion Polk Angellotti
Mark Overton
Mark Twain
Mary Austin
Mary Catherine Crowley
Mary Cole
Mary Hastings Bradley
Mary Roberts Rinehart
Mary Rowlandson
M. Wollstonecraft Shelley
Maud Lindsay
Max Beerbohm
Myra Kelly
Nathaniel Hawthrone
Nicolo Machiavelli
O. F. Walton
Oscar Wilde
Owen Johnson
P.G. Wodehouse
Paul and Mabel Thorne

Paul G. Tomlinson
Paul Severing
Percy Brebner
Percy Keese Fitzhugh
Peter B. Kyne
Plato
Quincy Allen
R. Derby Holmes
R. L. Stevenson
R. S. Ball
Rabindranath Tagore
Rahul Alvares
Ralph Bonehill
Ralph Henry Barbour
Ralph Victor
Ralph Waldo Emmerson
Rene Descartes
Ray Cummings
Rex Beach
Rex E. Beach
Richard Harding Davis
Richard Jefferies
Richard Le Gallienne
Robert Barr
Robert Frost
Robert Gordon Anderson
Robert L. Drake
Robert Lansing
Robert Lynd
Robert Michael Ballantyne
Robert W. Chambers
Rosa Nouchette Carey
Rudyard Kipling
Saint Augustine
Samuel B. Allison
Samuel Hopkins Adams
Sarah Bernhardt
Sarah C. Hallowell
Selma Lagerlof
Sherwood Anderson
Sigmund Freud
Standish O'Grady
Stanley Weyman
Stella Benson
Stella M. Francis
Stephen Crane
Stewart Edward White
Stijn Streuvels
Swami Abhedananda
Swami Parmananda
T. S. Ackland

T. S. Arthur
The Princess Der Ling
Thomas A. Janvier
Thomas A Kempis
Thomas Anderton
Thomas Bailey Aldrich
Thomas Bulfinch
Thomas De Quincey
Thomas Dixon
Thomas H. Huxley
Thomas Hardy
Thomas More
Thornton W. Burgess
U. S. Grant
Upton Sinclair
Valentine Williams
Various Authors
Vaughan Kester
Victor Appleton
Victor G. Durham
Victoria Cross
Virginia Woolf
Wadsworth Camp
Walter Camp
Walter Scott
Washington Irving
Wilbur Lawton
Wilkie Collins
Willa Cather
Willard F. Baker
William Dean Howells
William le Queux
W. Makepeace Thackeray
William W. Walter
William Shakespeare
Winston Churchill
Yei Theodora Ozaki
Yogi Ramacharaka
Young E. Allison
Zane Grey